"I never joke about sex," Cassandra declared

Noah didn't think he joked about sex either, but this took that to a whole other level. "Look, I don't mind about the condoms and the physical. That's good thinking, but the rest? It sounds like some sort of business arrangement."

"It is. Sort of. Sex is definitely business—don't let anyone tell you otherwise. I've never believed in masking it with all that lovey-dovey kitsch."

Noah had never thought of himself as a believer in romantic ideals, but now he felt sort of…insulted. "That lovey-dovey *kitsch* is the best part of a relationship." T kay, the sex is good row at that. "But you."

"Yes, I can."

Noah sighed. "You never compromise? You never make a promise, or ever stay faithful? What about the other rules?"

She shook her head and the dark hair brushed against her full breasts. What she was proposing was a one-night stand. A cheap roll in the hay. Wham, bam, thank you Noah.

Could he do it? How could he not?

Dear Reader,

Well, this is it. The last book in THE BACHELORETTE PACT miniseries. Cassandra's story. This one required a lot of thinking until I could get everything suited for who she really is. I knew the image that she reflected to the world, but the vulnerabilities, the darker parts that lurked inside her took a while to bring to the surface. Meanwhile the hero, Noah, just showed up right from Day One. He's the attentive man who's so smart that he sees through Cass's bravado from the start. Gotta love a man who's that bright. And this is their story.

I hope you've enjoyed the miniseries. Please write to me and let me know your thoughts at kathleenoreilly@earthlink.net or Kathleen O'Reilly, P.O. Box 312, Nyack, NY 10960.

All the best!

Kathleen O'Reilly

Books by Kathleen O'Reilly

HARLEQUIN TEMPTATION
 889—JUST KISS ME
 927—ONCE UPON A MATTRESS
*967—PILLOW TALK
*971—IT SHOULD HAPPEN TO YOU
*975—BREAKFAST AT BETHANY'S

*The Bachelorette Pact

HARLEQUIN DUETS
66—A CHRISTMAS CAROL

KATHLEEN O'REILLY

THE LONGEST NIGHT

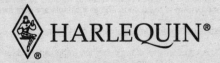

TORONTO • NEW YORK • LONDON
AMSTERDAM • PARIS • SYDNEY • HAMBURG
STOCKHOLM • ATHENS • TOKYO • MILAN • MADRID
PRAGUE • WARSAW • BUDAPEST • AUCKLAND

For my editor, Kathryn Lye.
I couldn't have done this without you.

ISBN 0-373-69179-3

THE LONGEST NIGHT

Copyright © 2004 by Kathleen Panov.

This edition published by arrangement with Harlequin Books S.A.

www.eHarlequin.com

Printed in U.S.A.

1

CASSANDRA WARD studied the subject in the chair, considering the shadows, the facets, and yes, even the flaws. But there was a beauty hidden inside, a beauty waiting to emerge, and now it was up to her, the artist at work, to expose it.

She took a step back, tracing slow circles at her temple while she considered the exact way to begin.

Carefully she adjusted the lights and watched the way the shadows fell. Thinking, analyzing, planning.

Finally it was time. As she smiled at Beth in the mirror, she cracked her knuckles. "You're going to look fabulous."

Beth frowned, obliviously not comprehending the talent that was at Cassandra's disposal. "I don't want to look like a tramp. I'm getting married today, not heading out for drinks."

Cassandra rolled her eyes, exquisitely made up in shades of silken taupe and almondine. "Does my makeup *ever* look trampish?"

Beth met her eyes in the mirror; she actually appeared to be thinking about it. "No," she answered at last.

They were alone in the church dressing room, two hours to the ceremony, and Cassandra was ensuring that one of her best friends was going to look beautiful.

She settled in to work. "Tell me why no one ever believes me."

First she dug into her makeup case and pulled out her secret weapon. Seaweed mask. "You're going to turn green, but don't worry. It'll exfoliate the skin and cleanse the pores, or exfoliate the pores and cleanse the skin. Not quite sure, but exfoliation and cleansing are definitely involved. You'll love it."

"After all that exfoliating and cleansing, I will return back to a normal skin color, right? What if I get some icky rash or something?"

"Trust me."

Beth sighed. "All right. Do your worst."

Cassandra spread the goo over Beth's face, covering the crucial areas in the T-zone. Then, while the mask was settling, she brought out her bag of cucumber slices and placed them on Beth's eyes. "This is to get rid of wrinkles. I buy cucumbers by the dozen."

Behind the cucumbers and seaweed, Beth laughed. "And here we thought it was for something else."

"Honey, there's no need for vegetables when able-bodied men are as close as the nearest speed dial."

While Beth was sitting in the chair, cucumbers on the eyes, face turning a healthy shade of green, Cassandra took out the extra two slices of cucumber and sat in the chair next to Beth. Just this morning she had noticed two new lines at the corner of her eyes. She didn't know if early onset of crow's feet ran in her family, but she wasn't taking any chances.

From the chapel area she could hear the pianist and the soloist practicing, some beautiful aria sung in a foreign language. Beth was going all-out for this wedding. Chicago would never see anything like this one again.

However, now the bride-to-be sat in the chair, quiet. Too quiet.

"Getting nervous?" Cassandra asked.

"*Mmm*, hmm."

"You shouldn't be. You're going to have the life you've dreamed up."

Beth worked her lips free of the mask. "No flowers or vacation on isolated beach."

Sometimes Beth didn't realize what she had. "He would if you asked him to."

"No fun."

"Wandering into the land of second thoughts?"

A smile cracked in the mask. "None."

"That's my girl."

There had been four bachelorettes at one time—four college friends, approaching thirty. They were single, they were happy, so they'd sworn to stay single forever. The Bachelorette Pact.

Cassandra frowned, which made for more wrinkles. She didn't frown often, but nobody was watching right now. Two bachelorettes were married, one was hours away from walking down the aisle.

And then there was one.

Cassandra "Eternally Single" Ward.

Not that she was complaining. Much. Jessica had married Adam, who was as big a competitor as she was, not that there was anything wrong with that. Mickey had married Dominic, an undercover cop who mingled with the dregs of Chicago society, and who needed that? Now Beth was marrying Spencer, a prize-winning journalist who, despite his love for Beth, still needed to learn some manners.

Her friends could have them all, because as far as Cassandra was concerned, the perfect man was nothing but a figment.

In the business of gems you had to spot the imperfections and cleave and saw and polish until all the flaws were gone. It was great for diamonds, but hell on men.

"You get married?" Beth said, struggling to talk through the quick-drying mask.

Cassandra shook her head, her nose filling with the scent of cucumber. "Never."

"You were go marry Benedict."

"I was young, impulsive...and stupid," said Cassandra.

Benedict O'Malley had taught her many things, most important among them, you can never escape who you are. She thought Benedict had seen something more than her body when he looked at her. Yeah, right. Cassandra was cheesecake—every man's favorite fantasy, so over the past eight years she'd perfected the fantasy into a fine art.

"Can't sex forever."

Insidious thoughts of falling boobs and lengthening crow's-feet crept into her mind, but today she was not going to feel sorry for herself. "Can, too," she answered, ripping the cucumbers from her eyes.

Beth shook her head.

It was a conversation they'd replayed many times. No one believed that Cassandra enjoyed her life. No one believed that a woman could indulge in sexual dalliances strictly for the pursuit of pleasure without any messy emotional complication. Yeah, well, no one knew what they were missing. No worries, no panicking about relationships torpedoing. No thank you, sex was strictly physical.

Cassandra practiced her own set of rules when it came to sex. Rule No. 1: no promises. That way she stayed disappointment-free. Rule No. 2: no option on exclusivity. If a man wanted an exclusive, he was shown the door. No man was worth that kind of loyalty. Rule No. 3: certain sexual behaviors were required, certain ones were allowed and certain ones were *verboten*. No threesomes, no dressing up in weird costumes and no bondage. Never bondage. Rule No. 4: a man must be factory inspected for disease. A piece of paper from the lab made it so much easier to keep things physical. And last, but most important, was Rule No. 5: no sex without Mr. Safety in place.

"I gonna fine you man," said Beth.

"Your mask is tightening up nicely. Just a few more seconds," answered Cassandra.

"You can hide."

"Time's up."

She warmed up a washcloth and began to wipe away the remains of the mask. Eventually, Beth emerged looking just as fresh-faced and glowing as normal, no crow's-feet, no laugh lines. By all rights, Cassandra should have hated her, but she didn't. Go figure.

"Now we're going to start with the base. Something pale for your complexion, but not cakey. Can't have you looking like the creature from the wax lagoon." She dug into her makeup box and brought out Powdered Bisque.

Beth sat still while Cassandra sponged on the base. But she knew that wouldn't last forever. And sure enough, Cassandra was right. "Spencer doesn't know many guys. There's Noah, but well, we already know *that* won't work out."

Cassandra stopped in midsponge. Just a moment, not enough for anyone to notice. She didn't want Beth to notice the telltale shaking in her hands. Steady, steady, steady. "Spare me from the Jimmy Stewart types." *The Jimmy Stewart types who had already shot her down once.*

"I'm going to talk to Jess and she'll talk to Adam. All those corporate types are connected, they know a lot of guys."

"Yeah, but they're all unemployed."

Adam was a reformed operational efficiency expert. He had been known as the "Ax-Man," before Jessica had turned him around.

Beth cast her a sharp look. "Well, what does that matter since you're not going to get serious anyway?"

Cassandra moved on to blush. Rose Shadows. "It doesn't. Why don't you leave my love life alone, hmm? I appreciate the thought, but I'm doing fine."

"It's wrong. There, I've said it. Morally, what you're doing is wrong."

Cassandra took a step back. It was a judgment she would have expected from Mickey, but never Beth, who didn't like to step on ants and had never swatted a mosquito in her life. "Why? I'm not getting married, so I'm expected to live like I'm stuck in some convent? Honey, my ticker is working just fine."

"I don't think it's wrong, you just make it so...cold-blooded. Sex shouldn't be that way."

"Men handle it just fine. It's all about the release. Nothing more. It's great exercise, clears up the complexion and relieves stress. Tell me how something that does all that *and* manages to make me feel good, could be bad for me?"

"I'm not saying it's bad for you," Beth started, then stopped. "Okay, I am, but why don't you try having a normal relationship for once?"

Cassandra snapped the blush case closed. "I wasn't built the way the rest of you were." It was true. She had the body of a stripper and men just didn't get "normal" female thoughts about her. She got the howlers, the whistlers, the grabbers and the droolers.

Beth met her eyes in the mirror. Her blond eyelashes were next on the list.

"Don't blame this all on your..." Beth couldn't bring herself to say it, so instead eyed meaningfully in the direction of Cassandra's chest. "Don't tell me you haven't had thoughts about getting a regular boyfriend. Don't you ever get lonely?"

No, she never got lonely, because she had perfected the art of being alone. "Let's move on to your eyelashes."

"I'm not done."

Cassandra shot her a hard glance. "I can put a mask on your mouth, too."

Beth held up a hand. The bride had finally remembered that today was supposed to be all about her. "Fine. Have it your way."

Cassandra pulled out the wand of mascara, soft brown, waterproof, because the last thing Beth needed to worry about was tears.

Cassandra didn't have to bother with waterproof. "No tears" was one of her rules, as well.

NOAH BARCLAY rolled in his bed, feeling the warm body right beneath his hands. She was there, her dark hair a thick curtain over her face. God, he loved her hair. He moved inside her, deep, deeper, and her legs tightened around his waist, taking him further inside. Then she smiled up at him and cocked her head. She was taunting him. He leaned down and kissed her, long and thorough, and when he drew back, she surprised him by pulling his head down again. This time she was biting his ear. Pleasure, pain.

He started to laugh. So she wanted to play? He could do that. He began to pound inside her, watching her dark eyes widen first with surprise, then pleasure. Her lashes were so long, thick, a mask she hid behind. He wouldn't let her hide from him. He brushed back the hair from her face, and still he pounded.

Pounded.

Pounded.

Damn!

Noah sat upright in his bed, the pounding noise still there.

What the hell?

He looked at his clock: 11:07. He'd slept in late this morning, but then, that was what happened when you returned from conducting business two continents from home.

Shaking off the remains of sleep, he pulled on a pair of boxers, noticed the swelling down below, then hastily reached for a pair of jeans, adjusting everything so that the pants would fit.

Back to reality. But, man, he wanted to go back to that dream.

For the past six months the dream had always been variations on a single theme: one beautiful woman, one desperate man and the kind of lovemaking that could bring a guy to his knees.

Noah gave himself a firm head-slap. Daylight was here, and there was an incessant knocking on his front door.

"What?" he snapped as he swung the door open.

It was Joan—the woman he normally called his sister. Today the label of choice was nuisance.

"You're not awake?" Joan asked, swaggering into his apartment with that awful perfume.

"Go away," growled Noah, thinking that if he didn't get too close to Joan, he could return to bed and finish the dream.

"You can't keep these sorts of hours, Noah. Look at you, circles under your eyes, and your hair, well, your hair looks terrible. You have a wedding tonight and I have a full list of items that I will need you to report on."

"I'm not going," he shot back, now sadly realizing that all hope of the fantasy replaying was gone.

She pulled her face into one long frowning line of disapproval. It was a look that he never fully appreciated until he'd cut through a camel market in his travels abroad. Definite similarities. "You have to go. You promised me."

"I said I would think about it. I did. No." He looked around the room. "God, I need coffee. Where's my coffee?"

"It's in your kitchen. For heaven's sake, wake up."

Noah glared and then wandered into the kitchen, trying to remember where he kept the coffeepot.

"You have to go," called Joan from the other room.

Noah put the coffee in the filter, rinsed out the pot, put it on the launchpad and then flipped the switch.

Nothing.

Well, what the—*water*.

He needed water.

He filled up the coffeepot, poured it through the top grid, then snapped the pot back in place. Happily, the gurgling started.

Eventually there was enough for a cup and he held it to his nose, inhaling the caffeine, letting it soak through his blood.

He wandered back into the living room, taking his first hit. Ah, much better. His blood started moving. He stared at Joan. Why was she here? Oh, yeah. The wedding.

"I have to know how many guests there are, the details of her dress, attendants, if you could get the name of the florist that would be wonderful, too," she intoned.

That was when he knew she'd read one too many bridal magazines.

"Aren't you over Spencer? You wanted the divorce. Hell, *you're* getting married, and Harry is really nice, by the way. Don't screw this one up."

"You think this is about Spencer?"

Noah took another sip of coffee. God, he really didn't need to have these conversations in the morning. "Yes."

"It's about *her*."

"Her?"

"Beth," she said, spitting out the name. "She wants the wedding of the season when I have the rightful claim. No way will she rob me. Spencer always told me, 'City hall, darling. It's romantic.' What does *she* get? Stained-glass windows by Tiffany and a caterer imported from New York. It's a war, Noah, and I'm going to win."

"I'm not going. Goodbye," he repeated, yet still not awake enough to open the door.

"Please," she said, using her wheedling tone, a tone she had used when they were little, and he would be the one to inevitably end up in trouble. It still bothered him.

"No."

"Most of Chicago's city council will be there, Noah."

Noah stopped. Okay, that was tempting. He had been trying to get onto the list of bidders for the new transportation project. For fourteen years he'd done construction work overseas, but this would be his first project in the U.S. His first project since he'd come home. "How would you know who's been invited?"

Joan smiled and lifted an eyebrow. "It only takes one well-greased request to the wedding planner and you'd be surprised what you can find out."

If it had been any other female, he would have been shocked. Unfortunately, Joan was his sister. His only sister. He knew her good qualities, her bad qualities and her worse qualities.

So, the city council would be there. Alderman Brown, Alderman Showalter and Alderwoman Weller among them. Spencer, aka the groom, covered the city beat for the *Herald* so it wasn't a surprise.

"Why don't you want to go?" asked Joan.

Noah shifted in his seat. "I don't like weddings," he said. It was a good answer, but not the right one. He didn't want to go because he knew exactly who would be there and that worried him.

Not the Chicago city council. Not the state of Illinois' biggest politicos. No, he was worried about one Cassandra Ward. The Windy City's original partygirl. Vamp extraordinaire, she could seduce a man with a single look. Breasts like B-32s, but it was her mouth that took on mythical proportions.

He had turned her down once and he wasn't man enough to do it again.

"The groom is your brother-in-law," Joan said, ripping him away from thoughts of long, leisurely nights with Cassandra.

"When you divorced him, he officially became not-my-brother-in-law."

Joan shrugged. "Don't split hairs. He's family. You need him."

What Noah didn't need was the raging erection he got every time he thought about Cassandra. And then there were the dreams. Wet dreams were supposed to stop with adolescence. Noah blamed it on lack of sex.

There were plenty of women available. All nice, all lookers, but they just didn't fire his blood. Six months ago Cassandra had ruined him for any other woman. If he saw her again, he'd be ruined for another six months. No woman was worth a full year of celibacy.

Damn.

He sighed, pulled out a tattered copy of the *Herald*, and pretended to read.

"So?" asked Joan, not taking the hint.

He knew he'd go, but he wasn't going to tell her yet. Let her worry. Noah wanted to make her pay. He was still ticked off about being woken up because he had really, *really* wanted to finish that dream.

THE SOLOIST was already singing when he slipped into the back of the chapel. Five minutes late wasn't so bad. The church was full. Five hundred heads or so, he guessed. Of course, according to Spencer, the bride had been planning this wedding for seventeen years, so it wasn't that much of a shocker.

The bridesmaids started down the aisle. Some new faces. Some not.

The first was cute and teary-eyed. Behind her was a tall, nervous-looking one in geeky glasses.

The last one was Cassandra.

They had put her in a demure dress, deep maroon, long sleeves, no cleavage. It wouldn't have mattered. The color made her hair darker, made her eyes more mysterious. She had kept her hair loose, falling in big curls to her waist. God, she could make a man want.

Currently, he wanted. He should have been terrified by the thought. One look in those deep pools of brown and a man turned to stone, or at least the important parts did.

Deliberately, Noah turned away and began to studiously examine the toes of his shoes. He had never been one to run with the pack, instead choosing his own way, and damn if he was just going to be another notch on her lipstick case.

He kept his eyes downcast as she walked past, but he didn't need to look to remember. He had every curve of that perfect body committed to memory.

Yeah, him and the rest of Chicago.

That was the big drawback to Cassandra. Her body was the sort that haunted men and she was the sort of woman who loved to act on it.

Not that he was going to judge her, but Noah had always been proprietary. What was his, stayed his, and all his life he'd stayed away from the girls who were busy on Friday nights. He knew men who had gotten burned by obsessing over Cassandra. Noah knew better.

He looked up and his hot gaze followed her as she walked down the aisle. But sometimes just knowing better wasn't enough.

THE RECEPTION was a beautiful thing, with a string quartet and a bubbling champagne fountain. Each table was covered with white daisies. Cassandra smiled from her table located in a back corner. The ceremony had been exquisite—the perfect mix of style and heart. Beth had cried like a baby, exactly like they had all known she would. Beth could be a sentimental fool, but Cassandra always had a soft spot for her anyway.

Mickey made her way across the room and sat down in an empty chair next to Cassandra. Mickey was not nearly as sappy as Beth, although sometimes the brainiac tortoise-shell lenses misted into a soft shade of rose. "What you doing?"

Cassandra pointed to her plate of desserts. "I'm eating my way to exercise class tomorrow."

Mickey snorted. "Hand me one of those," she requested, snagging a cream puff.

"You need to try the éclairs," said Cassandra, who believed that dessert belonged predinner rather than post. "Where's Dominic?"

Dominic was Mickey's husband and the subject of

a large percentage of Mickey's goofier moments. "He'll be here in a minute," she answered, polishing off the dessert. "Had to go and make a call. Why didn't you bring a date?"

"No one was worthy," offered Cassandra with a shrug. She hadn't brought a date to any of her friends' weddings. It didn't seem right. Her men fell into one category, her friends into another. And Cassandra didn't believe in category mixing.

"Off week, huh?"

"Never," she said, flashing her mysterious smile. She liked building upon the Cassandra mystique. And the more her best friends coupled up, the more Cassandra played it up. Maybe it was shallow, but she wanted to remind them that single life really did have its own rewards.

"There are some eligibles here, by the way. A couple of men from the *Herald*, plus, all Beth's waiters are here."

Cassandra scoped out the hotties who were tending bar and laughed at the familiar faces. Thomas, Seth and Charles. Beth had opened a tearoom, highbrow and staid, except for the waiters in tuxes that made it smolder, Chicago-style.

"They're just babes in the wood," answered Cassandra, though she had actually considered it at one time.

"Beth told me who Noah was. Quite conveniently we noticed that he's alone."

Cassandra tapped a fingernail on the table as her sole concession to Noah Barclay. "Why don't you go find your husband? I'll be fine."

"You don't want company?"

"It's nice to sit and think, remember all the good times we had."

"It's a wedding, not a funeral," said Mickey, using her glasses for the full egghead effect.

Cassandra leaned back, watching the matrimonial circus in front of her. "It all depends on your perspective."

2

IT SADDENED NOAH that his sister had been right. The James-Von Meeter wedding hosted a hotbed of Chicago politicos. So far he had discussed the finer points of a chocolate layer wedding cake with Alderman Frederick H. Brown from the Eighteenth Ward, not to be confused with Frederick T. Brown from the Fourth Ward. He'd asked Alderwoman Margaret Watson from the Twenty-second Ward to dance, only to discover that she was on crutches. And he'd rescued Judge Roscoe Warren from dunking his head in the punch bowl. Judge Warren was a two-fisted drinker, and not a steady one at that. It was a lot of work for Noah, who didn't feel comfortable mingling among the artificial ingredients of society.

Having had quite enough of that, Noah escaped to the relative safety of the bar. He watched Cassandra as she sat by herself, drinking a vodka martini. Judging from the vibration at her throat, he thought she might be humming.

It didn't seem normal to see her sitting there alone. In his mind, she was always surrounded by a pack of men as the goddess granting favors while the mortals genuflected at her feet.

Thoughts like that kept him firmly at the bar, nursing his whiskey.

At this rate he was going to end up with another three years of celibacy. God, six months had been bad enough. He sighed and deliberately turned away just as two men approached.

"I'm going to go see if she needs another drink," one said in a cocksure voice, with lust deep in his mortal heart.

Two guesses whom they were talking about.

"You think she'd let me take her home?" asked the shorter one, younger and less worthy of a good beating.

"She's drinking martinis, right? Load her down with a couple and you'll be on your way to paradise. Did you read about the time after the Blackhawks post-season party? I heard she was there."

Noah swallowed his drink, then swallowed the anger that rose in his throat. *Stay out of it. It isn't your place.*

As he watched, the two men made their way across the room to flirt with her. She laughed at some stupid joke. Probably a dirty one. But it was none of his concern.

While he kept his distance, she tilted back her

head, clearly having a great time. The next thing he knew, the tall man was handing her another martini.

Bastard.

He really didn't want to interfere; he'd wait until she sent them on their way.

The minutes ticked by and she didn't.

They were pricks on the prowl. Couldn't she tell? Well, for tonight, there was a new sheriff in town.

With his mind made up, he walked over to the table. His fantasies and his more noble aspirations started to merge until, in his mind, she was swearing her undying gratitude, even as he was ripping off her dress.

"Hello, Cassandra," he said, betting her golden-tanned skin was golden-tanned all over—it was in his dreams. While he was still contemplating the seductive vision, he realized he had nothing else prepared to say. He usually thought faster on his feet, instead, he was staring hot-eyed and openmouthed, just like the other two pricks on the prowl.

He wondered if she had forgotten that he'd once rejected her offer. He'd been polite, nice, but firm. And stupid.

Then she looked up, met his eyes square on, and he flinched at the ice he saw there. "Noah."

Okay, so she remembered. So maybe things were going to be a little more difficult than he'd planned.

"Do I get to meet your friends?" he asked, willing

to persevere because this was for her own good. Sorta.

Another cold smile. "Noah, meet Daniel and Bruce."

Noah held out his hand, which everyone ignored. "Nice to meet you gentlemen."

Bruce, the one with the flagrant hard-on in his eyes, just looked pissed. Too bad, buddy. Deal with it.

Noah looked at the empty chair on the other side of Cassandra. "You mind?"

She shot him a hell-yes look, but shrugged one languid roll of the shoulder. "It's a free country."

"So, Danny, what do you do?" he asked.

"Daniel."

"Daniel." *Dickhead.* "What do you do?"

"I work for the *Herald.* Sales."

"Are you in sales, too, Bruce?" asked Noah, who as a rule never liked salesmen anyway.

Bruce nodded, but didn't say a word.

Noah turned to Cassandra, content to cut the other two out of the conversation. "What's up in the lapidary business?"

"We cut, we grind, we polish, we sell. It's all the same, day in, day out."

Noah leaned on his palm. "I think that's fascinating. Don't you, guys? I mean, how do you know where to cut?"

She smiled at him, showing perfect white teeth. "I'm very good with a saw."

So, she wanted to make rescuing difficult. However, Noah was of the firm belief that sometimes people didn't know what was good for them. He pushed forward. "If I was in the market for a diamond, what advice would you give?"

"Go to South America."

God, he was a masochist.

Finally, Bruce couldn't take any more. "Listen, Noel—"

"It's Noah."

"Yeah, Noah, then. I'm not sure the lady's really interested in your company, if you get my meaning? Maybe you could focus your charm on someone else."

Noah coughed, indicating he was finished with polite games. "Isn't that the second martini, dickhead? Looks like you're no closer to paradise than you were when you started. In fact, I think you could give the lady thirty martinis and she still wouldn't go home with you."

Bruce got up, looking to intimidate. "It's not polite to easedrop, friend."

Noah stood and went chest-to-chest with the guy. Bruce was big, but Noah was bigger. "I'm being plenty polite, considering. And don't call me friend."

That finally brought a reaction from Cassandra. She straightened, the chin lifted and the cold, dark eyes fixed on Bruce and Danny-boy. "Get away. Now."

The men realized paradise was not the place for mortals and slunk back to the more earthly planes of the bar.

Noah, pleased to have finally gotten this rescue thing right, smiled and sat down, waiting for her word of gratitude.

"And you, too," she said, not sounding thankful at all.

"Excuse me? I thought you would at least thank me?"

"Thank you. Now please leave." She looked pale. Her sinful red lips were tightly pursed.

He wasn't ready to leave. Not yet. "You know, I could have just left things alone, let those two jerks ply you with alcohol and then damn the consequences, but I chose to interfere. Do you understand? I *chose to interfere* for you. I thought you might care."

The dark gaze lifted in his direction, but now her expression showed only fire. "You worried for no reason. No man takes advantage of me unless I want him to. I appreciate your *interference*, but I don't need it. Go practice your knight-errant shtick someplace else."

Now was the time to escape. *Go away, Noah, you're not invited here.* In fact, he started to get up, but then he sat back down because he was curious. "Don't you care?"

"About what?"

"The way people talk."

She looked up, her eyes empty and still. "The only person I hear talking is you."

Her complete isolation tugged at him. She looked so tough, so above everyone else. The goddess alone. Noah had always been surrounded by family, friends or by co-workers and had never stopped to wonder if he would like being alone. He didn't think he would.

"Can I keep you company?"

She raised a brow. "The word no seems to be a word you don't understand, so I'll save my breath."

"So...you're friends with Beth?" he asked. He already knew the answer to his question, and he knew that she knew he knew the answer to it, but the ice caps in her eyes were shrinking so he pressed ahead—Titanic-style.

She nodded and Noah continued.

"She seems nice. I don't know why she's marrying Spencer, but there's no accounting for taste."

Hesitatingly, her lips curved up. It wasn't much, but he labeled it progress. Soon, he'd have her right where he wanted her. It was only a matter of time.

"They get along well," she said quietly.

"I guess," he said as he studied her.

"If you'll excuse me, I've got a headache and I need to say good-bye to the bride before they go. Then I'm sneaking out, as well."

She was leaving?

She obviously hadn't read his plan for this relationship.

Hell, most women in the great state of Illinois would fight for his company. Noah didn't consider himself vain, just a realist. The Barclay name and the legendary bank accounts gave him an extra advantage that an ordinary man didn't have. And the fact that he had a full head of hair didn't hurt.

One thing his father had taught him about the Barclays: they always got what they wanted. Sometimes it took patience, sometimes it took money, sometimes it was a well-placed rumor and sometimes it was hard-earned luck. But they always got what they wanted, and Noah was a Barclay through and through. An easygoing smile could hide a lot.

"Go out with me," he heard himself say.

"You told me you weren't interested."

"I lied."

She studied her nails. "Lying will not score you points here."

"You know, I thought you might have trouble with that."

"Mr. Barclay, on any one night I have my pick of men to go out with—" Just then her cell phone rang. "Excuse me."

She pursed her lips, this time completely on purpose, and laughed into the phone. He listened while she cooed over "Christoph."

"Oh, honey, I can't tonight. Got this wedding thing. After? No. I don't do weddings well, so I think I'm heading home to wash the scent of honeysuckle and *amore* right off of me.

"Yes, alone," she said in a throaty whisper designed to send Christoph into fantasyland.

He took the phone away and hung up on Christoph.

She wasn't pleased. "That was rude."

"That was a marvelous performance."

"What do you mean?"

He shook his head and picked up her hand. Lovely skin. It was soft, her scarlet nails shone like water.

She started to pull her hand away, but he raised an eyebrow and her movements stilled.

"You don't do weddings, huh?"

"Too much sugar makes me nauseous."

"Go out with me."

"I'm sorry, but I believe your exact words were, 'You're a nice girl, but not tonight.'"

"I don't like being used," he said resolutely. Of

course, half a year without sex could melt the strongest resolution, but he wasn't going to tell her that.

"What's that supposed to mean?"

"Six months ago, how much of the tartlet performance at the gala was for my benefit and how much of it was to piss off your old boyfriend?" he asked.

"I don't do tartlet performances," she started. Though she didn't deny the piss-off-your-old-boyfriend part at all, which irked him, because he liked to think that on that one night six months ago she had felt the slow burn between them.

"Too old?" he questioned, mainly because he was irked.

Her dark brows furrowed in anger. He held up the hand of peace. "Apologies. You bring out the worst in me."

"An auspicious way to start a relationship, Mr. Barclay. I would think you'd be running hard and fast in the opposite direction. Some repressed need for self-punishment, perhaps?"

He balanced his chin on his hand, content to drink in her face. It was like pouring one-hundred-and-forty proof right onto his crotch. He'd never met a woman who was so completely aware of her own power.

"I'm not giving up," he said.

"Cocky, aren't we?" she asked with a cold look in her eyes that should have kept him away.

"Cocky? You've been stuck up here for the past six months," he said, pointing to his head. "I can't look at another woman, I can't sleep because of the dreams, and I didn't want to come tonight because I knew what would happen."

"What?" she asked quietly.

"It'll start all over again. You'll ruin me for another six months, only now, well, it's worse. So I'm thinking it's now going to be at least a year. Yeah, I see that smile. You think this is funny, but I don't. This is all about survival, sweetheart. Mine."

There. He'd told her. It wasn't the sophisticated approach he probably should've used, but he hadn't had much sleep lately and it was all because of her.

Then she got up to leave. He'd blown it. His one shot. Gone. She glanced around the room and cast one anxious glance in his direction. "The store. Tuesday," she whispered, and then quickly walked away.

ON SUNDAY MORNING, Cassandra was up early. She always squeezed in a workout before she started the day, but last night she'd had very little sleep, and it was all Noah Barclay's fault.

Everything had been fine until she'd looked deep into his dark, tortured gaze. This was a man who looked to be in pain, and she'd put him there. There was the usual victory dance of power in her head, but this time the victory dance wasn't nearly as much fun.

In fact, this time the victory dance was completely unfun.

It was that complete lack of fun that prompted her to give him a second chance. That, and the fact that the man had the most mesmerizing eyes. Honest and completely unsmarmy. She'd actually checked. But there was no telltale hand over the mouth or the shifty-eyed marker of dishonesty. He'd met her gaze square-on and she'd gotten a jolt that she hadn't been expecting.

Okay, sue her, she was attracted to the man. She would give him a shot, then he'd show his true colors and, yeah, she'd seen the end of this movie before.

Cassandra picked up her mop from the broom closet and jabbed at the floor with more anger than precision. Nothing like a little housework to ease frustration.

She lived in a little, two-bedroom, one-tiny-bath, no-garage in Hardwood Heights. It was her sanctuary and she loved it. The community had strict rules about noise and behavior, so it was always quiet. Peaceful.

So peaceful that it was unnervingly loud when she heard a scratching noise at the front of her house.

That was odd, she thought as she peered through

the glass in her front door. No one was there. But then the scratching started again.

She flung open the door. Still nothing.

Then she looked down.

Some people might have called it a dog. Cassandra was horrified, and slammed the door on it.

She hated dogs.

The scratching started again.

Her fingers drummed against the wood door frame, knowing that if that stupid animal didn't stop, her brand-new, seven-hundred-and-eighty-six-dollar door was going to be ruined. It was a honey, too. Golden oak with beveled glass that just dressed her place up so nicely.

No way was that dog going to ruin it.

She marched to the kitchen and filled a pitcher with water. Then she opened the door and doused him.

The mutt retreated to the lawn and sat on his haunches, fur bunched and smelly—now a wet smelly—and glared back.

"You're a stupid dog, aren't you?"

She slammed the door and waited. The scratching started again.

Darn it. He wasn't leaving.

Where did the thing belong? Maybe a neighbor had lost it? Not that she thought anyone was going to claim it. Something that huge and that old and that ugly wasn't going to be popular anywhere. Worst of all, it had big, mean teeth.

After gathering her courage, she threw on some shoes and went outside. She was prepared to confront the monster, using the back door of course.

She clapped her hands in what she thought was an anti-dog manner. "Go home."

The dog growled at her.

Okay, let's try something new. Kindness. "Here, buddy," she sang, snapping her fingers.

The dog growled at her.

"You are a stupid, stupid animal," she announced, and the dog promptly went and curled up on her porch. Not that her porch was large, mind you. In fact, the dog took up the entire space.

"No, no, no. You belong to someone else. This is not your home. Bad dog, bad dog."

The dog opened one lazy eye and showed his teeth in a twisted-looking grin.

"Where's Timmy, boy?"

The dog yawned.

Okay, this was getting her nowhere. She gave him the eye as she walked next door to Mrs. Mackenzie's place. Mrs. Mackenzie was an elderly woman who, to Cassandra's knowledge, had no pets, but maybe that had changed. After all, it was never too late to gain a pet.

When Mrs. Mackenzie answered her door, Cassandra smiled politely. "Did you lose a dog?" she asked with hope in her voice.

Mrs. Mackenzie squinted, her mind creaking. She was a dear old woman, but a little slow. "No. Can't say that I did."

"Do you know anyone in the neighborhood who's lost a dog recently? Big, ugly, black and gray."

Mrs. Mackenzie shook her head. "No, dear. The neighborhood board frowns on dogs. Don't know anyone around here that has one. Sorry. Would you like some pie? I just made a fresh cherry. With ice cream."

Cassandra shook her head, depressed at the fifty-pound spawn of Satan that had just been dumped in the lap of her lawn.

Still determined, she went door to door, covering thirty-seven houses in five blocks. And all she got for her trouble was seven chocolate-chip cookies and three lewd propositions. Damned perverts. Somebody out there was dog-less, probably crying and worrying.

She made her way home, munching the last cookie, thinking that maybe the animal had disappeared while she was gone. No such luck. As she rounded the corner, there he was, curled up in a big, ugly black ball on her porch. At least he had stopped the scratching. She stood at the end of her walkway, considering her approach. She really didn't like dogs.

This one growled, showing really big teeth.

"Shoo. I'm going inside now."

The dog ignored her.

"I'm walking to the door now," she said, taking two slow steps.

The dog still ignored her.

"I'm coming closer. Don't upset me, dog, or you'll be sorry."

The dog opened one sleepy eye.

Two more steps and he began to growl.

"Don't mess with me." And almost, almost, almost...

He jumped to his feet and started barking.

Not.

She blew out a breath and stared the dog down.

He glared back, showing more teeth. God, she hated those teeth.

As she made her way to the back door, she cursed all dogs, cursed all dog puppies, and decided that immediately when she made it to safety, she was calling Animal Control.

When she walked into the living room, she glanced outside. Spawn was still there.

"Fine. It's your doggie hide." She looked up the number for Animal Control, dialed, and got a recording. Due to budget constraints, they were closed on Sundays. So she left her name and number and hung up.

Then she opened the front door and yelled at the animal. "I'll say this for you, you're one lucky dog. You've got twenty-four hours and then the police are coming for you, Spawn."

The dog lifted his big head and growled.

"If you think I'm going to feed you, you're nuts."

Later, after the sun had gone down, she peeked outside, just to see if he was still there. There he was, sleeping the deep sleep of the innocent—while trespassing on her property. He looked kind of thin, though, so she crept outside to look closer. She should feed him. Bad nutrition could cause all sorts of problems, like poor skin and weak bones. And Animal Control would be here in the morning and they'd take him away, so what harm was there in giving the mutt some food.

He didn't stir when she approached and she noticed his ribs clearly showing through. Anorexic dog. Then she bent and put the rice cakes and chips on the ground. Not that close, cause she still didn't trust him. Just as soon as she was done, she ran back inside.

After she left, the dog opened one eye and stared. Then he wolfed down the food and just as quickly went back to sleep.

ON MONDAY MORNING, Animal Control appeared before Cassandra had even done her makeup, so she shoved a baseball cap on and pulled it low. Spawn was still happily curled on her porch, oblivious to his impending doom.

The Animal Control guy, Gus, was very nice. Cassandra asked him all sorts of questions about what would happen with the dog, merely because she was ignorant about how these things worked. Spawn had a thirty-day shot at adoption and, if he was voted off the island, then they'd put him to sleep.

It seemed harsh, but the city was cutting back. She considered the big monster, realized that if there was an island castoff, he was it. Nobody would adopt this dog. Finally she shook her head. He didn't deserve this, not with those teeth, and his owner could still be out there, searching.

"Let him stay here for now."

Gus frowned. Obviously he didn't like having his power of life and death usurped. "You'll have to get him shots and tags. It's illegal for him to be without them. And watch the noise. Too much barking and I'll be back."

She smiled and easily summoned a thousand watts of sexuality—guaranteed to weaken the strongest man's will, even without her makeup. "I'll take care of it today, assuming that I can get in to see a vet."

"There's a new place on Cedar Avenue. They'll do him. And Tuesday night he stays open until nine. If you decide to keep him, get him neutered. Pet population—it's all our responsibility."

She tugged at the brim of her cap. "Of course. Thank you for your help, Gus. Sorry to have dragged you out here for nothing."

"You brightened my day, ma'am. That's enough."

After the Animal Control truck pulled away, Spawn lifted his massive head and eyed her.

She narrowed her gaze. "Don't think I was being nice, you understand? You've got twenty-four hours to find your owner. Twenty-four hours, that's it. After that, you're on your own."

FOR THE FIRST TIME in her thirteen years in the diamond biz, Cassandra was the sole proprietor of Diamonds by Ward & Ward. Jozef Ward, her father, had left for the summer. His destination: the lake cabin in Minnesota. Thereby leaving Cassandra solely in charge. His last words before he left were, "Don't let the power go to your head. I'll be back."

Before he'd gone, Jozef hired Kimberly for the summer help. Heavy accent on the word "summer" and light on the word "help." The girl had brains, her father wouldn't have hired her otherwise; however, Kimberly also had attitude in spades. And if Cassandra hadn't felt minor sympathy for her—the girl was a fashion train wreck—she would have fired her after two weeks.

Cassandra dug under the papers on the counter, searching through the notepads that had been so nicely organized before she'd taken her day off. Her *one* day off, thank you very much. Then she came back and everything was a mess.

"Kimberly, did you see the notes I took for Mr. Amesworth? He's got an appointment on Thursday and I wanted to pick out a few stones for him."

"Did you check on the counter?"

Did you check on the counter? Cassandra mimed to the god of patience. "Yes, I did."

"Haven't seen it," yelled Kimberly from the back.

"Can you help me look for it?"

Kimberly appeared in the doorway to the front area, in full confrontational stance with her fists on hips and jaw set tight. It was more pity than fear that struck Cassandra. She shook her head at the loose brown shirt, faded brown jeans and wiry brown hair. The girl needed a renewed body outlook, that was for sure.

"I haven't seen it. By the way, Mr. Liepshutz was by yesterday, looking for you."

Cassandra stopped looking. She didn't like Sidney Liepshutz. Didn't want to be alone with Sidney Liepshutz and Kimberly knew it. Kimberly smiled a screw-you smile. "I told him you'd be working to-day."

Cassandra was about to start yelling when the door buzzer sounded and a construction worker came in. Mark, Matthew—he had some "M" name that Cassandra had forgotten. The twenty-two-year-old boy-toy had developed a crush. On her.

He doffed his hard hat, a rather sweet gesture, and coughed. "Miss Ward, I just wanted to tell you that we'll be working on the water lines again today."

Which translated to: the power was going to be cut. "How long will you be working today?"

"All day, ma'am," he said. "I'm sorry. I know this is hard on you."

"I'm sure I'm not the only one," she said with a faux smile. The last thing she needed was for the power to go out. The store's locks were electronic and when there was no power, there was no business. She turned, ready to ask Kimberly about the appointments for the day, but Kimberly wasn't paying attention to Cassandra. No, Kimberly was in a trance. Change that to starstruck. She was starstruck at the sight of Mark, Matthew or whatever the boy's name was.

Interesting. She looked almost nice when she was in the throes of lust.

Every woman had her weakest point, usually tied

to a man, and finally Cassandra had found one in Kimberly. Mark, Matthew or whatever.

"Kimberly," said Cassandra, and Kimberly jerked out of her reverie.

"Yes?"

"Can you get Mr. Pipe Fixer some water? And be quick about it. It hit ninety degrees yesterday. Whew. These summers can be hot." She drew a hand over her forehead for effect. "I'm going to check in the back for the order form."

"His name is Mark," grumbled Kimberly.

"Oh, yes." Cassandra glowed in Mark's general direction. "Suck up some air-conditioning, Mark," she said, and then disappeared. "I have to work."

She plastered herself to the door and then listened to Kimberly's monosyllabic tones, shaking her head. The conversation was about as scintillating as the stock market report. Eventually Mark disappeared—a less sensitive woman would have said "ran"—the electric door beeping behind him.

Kimberly slunk into the back room, shoulders drooping, traditional rejection pose.

For a second, only one short second, Cassandra identified with Kimberly. Women could be such suckers for men.

Finally, she sighed. What would it hurt? "You know, we could make a deal," said Cassandra.

"What sort of deal?"

"You want Mark?"

"No," the girl said, lying through her teeth.

"I can help you there, if you'll help me."

"I don't need your help."

Cassandra knew that laughing wouldn't advance her cause, so she choked it down her throat. "Can I tell you something, woman to woman?"

Kimberly shrugged her shoulders, an ungainly move that accentuated her bad posture.

"You could have him eating right out of your hand."

"Not in this lifetime," said Kimberly, dripping sarcasm.

"I'm serious."

"Uh, no. I don't look like you, Miss Ward."

And how it must have pained her to admit that. Cassandra shook her head again. "It's all about the illusion, Kimberly. How you look has very little to do with it."

"I don't want your help."

Cassandra went on, "Do you know how many people have asked me my secret? Tons. I could have my own infomercial and make a mint, but it's no good if you tell everyone what it is. But here I am, offering you a gesture of friendship, offering to share my most valuable insights regarding the weaker sex, and you're turning them down. I think that's rude, Kimberly."

"I don't want to be rude," muttered Kimberly.

"I didn't think so. You're not the type. Let me help you."

"You just feel sorry for me."

"Maybe. But I need your help this summer, and I don't want to have to tippy-toe around the store, trying to figure out what to say, what not to say, it'd be *très* awkward. This is my first summer in the store alone, and I need to keep things in order while Dad is gone. You can understand that, can't you?"

Kimberly shrugged.

"We'll start with the basics today. Flirting and Body Language 101. Tomorrow I'll bring in some clothes and makeup."

"You really think you could turn me into something else?"

Cassandra dragged Kimberly over to the mirror and planted her in front. "Smile.

"Now pull up your chin—

"Shoulders back—

"One foot in front of the other—

"Hand on hip, fingers splayed—

"Now what do you see?" Cassandra asked.

"I *do* look better."

"It's nothing but confidence. It's the most potent weapon in a woman's arsenal, so don't leave home without it. Now go out to the front and find the order from Mr. Amesworth."

"But I don't know where it is!"

Cassandra shook her fingers. "Nuh-uh-uh. Shoulders back, chin up. Just remember, confidence."

DIAMONDS by Ward & Ward was on Wabash Street right in the middle of Jeweler's Row. It was Chicago's very own version of 47th Street. Window after window was filled with fiery gold and diamonds. Diamonds that could fill a woman's eyes with tears just as fast as they could empty a man's bank account.

Noah walked in, expecting, hoping to see Cassandra; instead he found a frumpy female digging through papers.

"Is Cassandra here?"

She held up a hand and pulled out a document from the bottom of the pile. "Aha! Got it. Wait a minute. I'll get her."

Noah didn't quite follow that, but he stayed silent as the girl disappeared into the back.

While he waited, he looked in the display cases, noticing the myriad stones that winked back at him. Most were set in rings or bracelets, but some had been scattered loosely on velvet-covered trays. White diamonds, red diamonds and yellow diamonds.

When he lifted his head, she was there, framed in the doorway.

Noah had to hand it to her—the woman could make an entrance. Her low-slung jeans were just a hair shy of decency, hugging centerfold curves. She wore a simple long-sleeved shirt. If any garment that hugged that magnificent chest could be considered simple. They were clothes you'd see every day on the streets of Chicago, but no other clothes sent him from flaccid to rock-hard in under three seconds flat.

He coughed.

"Mr. Barclay. I'm surprised you remembered the invitation."

"Surely we've progressed beyond last names?"

"Noah."

He liked the way she said it, almost a whisper, her perfect mouth caressing his name. Her eyes looked softer today. The anger was gone. It was a good sign.

"Do a man a favor?" he asked.

The perfect mouth pulled into a tight line and the eyes grew sharp. He had a feeling that Cassandra Ward, society-page sex kitten, had taken his comment the wrong way. Oops. He was ready to apologize, but just as he opened his mouth, the sharpness was gone—like it'd never been there at all.

Her laugh was throaty and full, and her nails raked his hand—a teasing touch. "Hold that thought. I need to write something down before I forget." Then she pulled a pen from the drawer and leaned down on the counter, and Noah found himself staring in the valley of her breasts. A man could lose his soul there if he wasn't careful.

She scribbled down some notes. There was a name he couldn't read. Then she straightened, pen in one hand.

"Now. What sort of favor were you thinking of?" she asked, capping the pen and pointing it at him.

Noah swallowed. He had been ready to ask her to lunch, but she was fogging his brain.

"Something with just the two of us?" she asked, her eyes focused directly on his mouth, and he wondered where that girl was and why she wasn't rescuing him. He knew this was a bad idea, but he couldn't think rationally. All he could focus on was the liquid plumpness of her mouth and the thousand years of sin that were reflected in her eyes. Already he had a hard-on, a couple more seconds and he was going to explode.

She smiled at him, reading his thoughts, and leaned a hip against the counter, which meant six inches closer to him. And six inches closer to touching him. Then she slid the pen deep into the V of her shirt and he watched as it disappeared between sun-kissed skin. He licked his lips, and just when he was ready to go diving for the pen, she pulled it back out, tilted her head back and laughed.

Noah swallowed. Her laughter had been a little

too forced and he was hit with the uncomfortable re-
alization that he had just been played.

"You have all sorts of tricks stashed down your
shirt, don't you?"

The dark eyes flashed at him, the pen no longer
useful, so she put it down on the counter. "What do
you mean?"

"You know what I mean," he said, the carnal fog
starting to ease. It made him mad that he'd spent the
last six months aching for a woman who didn't even
exist.

"You want to sleep with me, don't you?"

"That thought was there, but I'm not your own
personal power switch to be flipped on when you're
in the mood to play."

She folded her arms across her chest and looked at
him. Finally, she nodded. "I have rules. First, no
promises, either given or taken. Second, you have to
agree with a medical inspection. Third, condoms are
required. Fourth, no monogamy. You see who you
choose and so do I. Lastly, no bondage. No explana-
tion necessary and if you need one, it's not going to
work between us anyway."

Noah's hard-on withered and died. "No monogamy? You've got to be kidding."

She didn't even smile. "Sex is a serious business.
And by the way, if I'm not coming, I'm going, if you
get my meaning. Sometimes it's there, sometimes it

isn't, but I'm not wasting my time if it isn't happening."

Then he understood. She was still pissed at him, and this was the price he was going to have to pay. Her own little practical joke. Okay, he deserved this.

"All right, all right, you got me. Look, I'm sorry about the six months ago. I told you I was stupid. You can understand why I had my doubts, but I'm over that now."

She stared at him blandly. "What does that have to do with anything?"

He lifted his hands. "You know. The joke, making me pay for what happened at the gala."

"I don't do revenge, Mr. Barclay. It's another time-waster. Those are my rules."

As he watched her and noted the steady state in her eyes, he realized this was serious. She was serious. "You're not joking?"

"No. I never joke about sex."

He didn't think he joked about sex, either, but this took that to a whole other level. "Look, I don't mind about the condoms and the physical. That's good thinking, but the rest? Excuse me, that sounds like business, not sex."

"I don't charge money, if that's what you're asking. But sex is definitely a business. Don't let anyone tell you otherwise. I don't believe in hiding behind all that touchy-feely kitsch."

Noah had never thought of himself as a touchy-feely believer himself, but now he was insulted. "That touchy-feely *kitsch* is the best part of a relationship." Then he realized what he'd said. "Okay, the sex is important, too—" she raised her brow "—but you can't just rip out all the other stuff."

"Yes, I can."

Noah sighed. This was going nowhere. "You never compromise? You'd never make a promise, or ever stay faithful?"

She shook her head and the dark hair brushed against her breast, but he kept his eyes glued firmly to her face.

What she was proposing was a one-night stand. A cheap roll in the hay. Wham, bam, thank you, Noah, good night.

So why was that a problem?

Maybe it was the ten years he'd spent overseas, maybe he was old-fashioned and never guessed it, or maybe it was because he wanted to be the one who was different.

She aroused him, and fascinated him, and intrigued him. He'd never met a sexier woman, never met a woman so assured. And now he realized that he'd never met a woman who thought so little of herself.

So now he just needed a new plan. A way to differentiate himself from the pack, and he knew there was a pack. His looks weren't going to cut it, his name didn't seem to mean a hell of a lot to her either, but he did have one other idea. A painful yet effective one.

"I tell you what. These rules are for sex. Intercourse. The old in-out, in-out, right?"

She nodded.

"Let's go back a step," he said.

"Excuse me?"

"What if all we're talking about is kissing?"

The finger-tapping started on the counter. "I don't like this."

"But consider, for the sake of argument, that I'm not interested in sex."

She shot him a skeptical look.

"I said for the sake of argument. What if you took a break for a little while?"

"Are we talking sex or kissing?"

"Kissing." He held up a hand. "Hear me out. This is good, this is great. You take a vacation, a time-out. You know, a breather? Just to relax, gain a little perspective, on the whole touchy-feeling ...junk."

Her eyes narrowed, so he started talking faster.

"And I will, too."

"That's monogamy," she retorted.

"But if I'm willing to sacrifice myself and forgo the heavy, *heavy* pleasures of carnal knowledge, shouldn't you?"

She shook her head. "It just means you're an idiot."

"Tell me how many other men have come to you and been willing to give up sex. I'm betting it's a big zero."

She was starting to smile. "It's not usually what I get propositioned with."

"Give me a shot. Give us a shot."

"I don't do 'us,'" she said, making a big production out of examining her nails.

"You know, so far, I've heard just about everything you don't do. Those rumors are overrated, aren't they?" he said, getting his hopes up.

She grinned, dashing his hopes right to the ground. "Nope."

Her cell phone rang and she picked it up from behind the counter. "Yes? Martin!"

Martin?

"Tonight? No can do. I've got a dog to take care of."

"Don't laugh."

"Maybe tomorrow," she started.

Noah pulled the phone out of her hand and cut off Martin as well.

"Now listen, you can't keep doing that."

"Stop answering your phone when I'm around and the problem's solved."

"No."

"I should leave, shouldn't I?" he said, knowing that he wasn't going anyway.

She nodded. "You're wasting your breath."

"What if you end up missing out on something?"

"I won't," she said stubbornly.

He stared at her, beginning to see below the surface. "Yeah, you will."

She rolled her eyes. "You're that good?"

"No, this isn't about me, or sex, or the almighty O. This is about you. It's about a man and a woman who can have a good time, a great time, an extraordinary time while not having sex. Haven't you just wanted to be around someone, just to see the way they smile, or try out a joke on them to see if it's as funny as you think it might be, but you're not sure." He started to get wound up. "Do you ever go out on a date just to be with a man? Just because he's someone you want to waste time with?"

She frowned and shook her head.

He had run out of things to say. He had run out of good arguments, and maybe she was right. He was wasting his breath. He turned around, ready to leave, even took a step to go, but he couldn't walk away from her.

He couldn't take another six months. He would be dead.

So he climbed from chair, to counter, and then hopped over the other side.

And before she could yell, he was kissing her. Noah believed in the All-American Kiss, but he'd never had to stake his future on one. She was tied to him in some way that he couldn't begin to understand.

His hands held her face just so. He was careful and cautious because this was all about seduction and not sex. At first she was surprised, he could feel the stiffness in her mouth, in her body. He pulled her closer, enfolded her in his arms and kissed her with everything he had.

3

CASSANDRA KEPT WAITING. She waited for the hands to creep under her shirt, waited for the practiced slide to the floor, but Noah surprised her.

She was being thoroughly kissed—and that was all. Eventually, she stopped the analysis and gave herself up to the simple pleasure of a kiss.

Good God, had it really been so long ago?

He lifted his head, his eyes dark and glazed. She loved that he got so drunk just from a single kiss.

"Please," he said.

She knew what he was asking. He wanted everything that she refused to give up. He wanted fidelity and promises, and all that went with it.

Maybe she felt a little drunk, as well, because she nodded.

"Go out with me tonight."

"I can't. I have to take a dog to a vet."

"I'll go with you."

She wanted time to regroup before she saw him again. He was pressing his advantage, and that made her uncomfortable. "It's a vet."

"I can help," he said, his eyes drifting down to her mouth, and a sharp punch hit her right between the thighs. What could it hurt?

"I would love it if you came with me. But you have to be careful. He bites."

Noah smiled. "So do I."

She gave him a sharp look and he looked moderately contrite.

"I know, I know," he said, hands raised. "But we don't have to worry about that now, either. I'll see you tonight."

His mouth quirked at the corners and he turned to walk out the door, the buzzer beeping behind him.

Her body, tired from all the tension that was shooting through her, sagged, and she made herself breathe.

Just as she was about to head back for the room, her cell rang.

It was Mickey.

"Is my name Martin? I don't think it's Martin. I think it's Michelle. Michelle, Martin. One's M-I, one's M-A. Not even close. And why did you hang up?"

"Sorry, Mick. Slight need-a-guy emergency."

"Find another *guy*, thank you very much. I have problems with my feminine image. You know that."

"Okay, okay, apology, apology. So what's up?"

"I've got the night free. Want to go listen to a lecture at the lab? I've got two tickets."

"No."

"Oh, come on. I'll go with you to Brick's afterward. Buy you a drink. And dessert."

"No."

"Why not? Dessert always works."

"I have plans."

"Tell him you'll go another night. You know how rare this is? It's Dr. Gruzinov, speaking on neutralinos. Trust me, it'll be astounding. You wouldn't believe the stuff they're doing with dark matter these days."

"No," said Cassandra, worrying that she was actually looking forward to seeing Noah. Okay, maybe she was hoping the dog would bite him, too, but that was just because he had turned her down once.

"Is this a date?" asked Mickey.

"I'm going to the vet."

"Getting spayed?"

"Spawn needs shots."

"Who is Spawn?"

"A dog."

"When did you get a dog?"

"Sunday. He's a stray."

"You took in a stray? God, Cassandra, he could have rabies. Have you had him tested? Those shots are murder. It's like a shot with horse needles, once a week, in the stomach, for a whole year."

"He doesn't have rabies. I don't think so, anyway." Spawn didn't foam at the mouth, he just slobbered a lot. "What if I drive out to Schaumburg tomorrow? We'll have a drink out on your side of town?"

Mickey sighed. "I can't believe I'm getting stood up for a dog. Cassandra you're getting boring."

She wasn't getting boring, she was just...trying out new things. After she hung up with Mickey, she called out to Kimberly. It was time for her first lesson, and Kimberly was lucky, because today Cassandra was feeling damn good.

"Okay, we've gone over the posture. Now I'm going to show you some signals you can use, or signals a man might give off."

Kimberly looked skeptical.

Cassandra smiled. "I know, but you have to trust me. You can use your eyes, your mouth, your hands or your body to signal what you're thinking, and best of all, you don't have to say a thing."

"I'm not very good at talking."

"Trust me, you'll be fine."

It turned out to be a great day. Kimberly sold two rings, actually got a smile out of Mark, and the power only went out three more times.

And then there was that kiss.

A less confident woman might have been nervous, might have been afraid of such an all-out, in-your-face specimen of masculinity. Cassandra ran a finger over her lips, secretly pleased by the aftershock that was still lingering inside her.

Bring it on, baby. Bring it on.

THE TRIP TO THE VET started innocently enough. Cassandra discovered that Spawn liked riding in the car. Wisely she chose to let Noah drive. Dog hair could do unmanageable things to silk and linen, and car upholstery, and if Noah was going to be chivalrous, well, there was a price.

When they arrived, Dr. Stevens introduced himself. He was young, just starting out in a new practice. And then, there was the added dimension of Dr. Stevens, Man on The Make.

Cassandra smiled grimly.

Oh, well. Better for Noah to understand the life of 36C cup right up-front.

Dr. Stevens asked questions about the dog, and she filled out the paperwork as best she could, considering the dog's history was a blank slate. Noah and the good vet got the beast on the table.

Eventually, it happened though. Okay, maybe she used her special smile on the good doctor, but it was only once, and he had given Spawn an extra treat, and whoops, it kinda slipped out, and she wasn't doing monogamy anyway. She had stated her opinion most emphatically.

"So you must be new in the area?" he asked.

"No," answered Cassandra politely, being careful to avoid eye contact.

"The dog is new," added Noah.

"The dog is old," said Dr. Stevens, obviously a believer in literality. "Your husband is good with him," fished Dr. Stevens, just as he was preparing to stick a needle into Spawn.

Cassandra looked away, not liking the idea of needles. "He's not my husband."

"Oh," said Dr. Stevens, his smile turning up a notch.

Cassandra looked at Noah, waiting for the traditional "marking of territory."

"Something wrong?" he asked her blandly.

She frowned, trying to figure his angle. "No."

"I don't mean to step on any toes, but I'm new to Illinois, just moved up from Texas, and if you're amenable, maybe we could have dinner sometime?"

Cassandra glanced over at Noah, waiting for him to blow, to say something, but instead he was watching her, one eyebrow raised.

In ordinary circumstances she would have said yes and then discreetly slipped the good doctor her phone number, whether she intended to go out with him or not. It was a wonderful method of keeping the males firmly in their place. Never let a man know that you're his.

However, Noah had popped up in a new place all by himself. He hadn't jumped right into sex, even though she knew how much he wanted her. So here she was—stuck. If she said no to Dr. Stevens, then she'd be going against all her principles. If she said yes, then would Noah disappear from her life? She had a feeling he would, and all her plans for hot sex would disappear, as well. Poof. Not fun.

She looked from Dr. Stevens back to Noah. "I have a rule against dating people who I do business with. It just muddies the water." Okay, it was a new rule, but it worked.

"He's only your vet," said Noah, smiling a cruel smile. "It's only your dog that he's doing business with, and that's temporary. Since you're not keeping the dog."

"Whose side are you on?" she asked.

"I thought you were antimonogamy."

Dr. Stevens began to look uncomfortable. "You know, maybe this was a bad idea."

Noah held up his hands. "No, no, if you want to date her, I think you should have that right."

Cassandra frowned. "If you'll excuse me, I always get nervous in doctor's offices." And then she ran.

ON THE DRIVE BACK to her house, she stayed quiet. Noah considered gloating, even prying gently, but that would probably be bad form and he had a feeling she would kick him in the opposite direction. Instead he turned up the radio, just enough to drown out the sound of Spawn's heavy breathing in his ear.

He glanced over and watched Cassandra a minute. She was tense, and nervous, her fingers tapping on her bag.

"He seems to have gotten over the shock," said Noah, just to make her fingers stop.

Cassandra looked in the back seat. "Sorry, boy. You live with me, you get your shots."

"You're going to keep him?"

"No," she said, no hesitation at all.

"What if nobody claims him?"

"Somebody will claim him," she answered, deep from the land of denial.

"They could have dumped him on your door," he said, needing to express his own suspicion.

"As the person least likely to take in a dog, they'd be pretty stupid to do that."

Noah pulled up in front of her house and walked around to open her door. She hopped out, followed by Spawn.

"Damn, that is one ugly dog."

The dog growled and then found his favorite spot on the porch.

"I think he's sensitive," she said.

"Yeah, I can see sensitive there. Do you mind if I come in?" Noah asked. He had waited all night to touch her.

She raised a brow. "Already changing your mind about this...taking-a-breathing stuff?"

Oh, she really had a low opinion of him, but that was okay. She was going to learn soon enough. "No, but it's still early. We could order a pizza, watch a movie and make out on the couch."

She laughed nervously. "I haven't made out on the couch since I was twelve."

"A woman is never too old to be kissed."

Noah reached out and took a lock of her hair in his fingers, playing and teasing. She had the most beautiful hair. Someday he was going to see it long, loose, hanging low over her breasts, but not tonight.

He sighed. "We don't need to rush, there's something to be said for a nice, slow seduction."

She shook her hair, so the strand in his fingers came free. "Dream on," she said, and then he watched as she walked to the steps, stared at the dog, and then shook her head. "We can go around back."

She really was the stuff that dreams were made of, and someday he was going to make her realize that.

NOAH MANAGED to persuade/bribe Spawn out to the backyard. It wasn't very big, but it had a fence, and finally Spawn seemed to understand that this was home. Noah watched while Cassandra laid out some food.

Rice cakes and potato chips.

"That's not dog food," Noah said as they walked inside the house.

"I'm not going to buy dog food."

"Don't you have hot dogs or meat or something?"

"No," she said, like he was an idiot.

Noah gave up. Tomorrow he'd buy her some dog food.

She came and sat down next to him, about two feet away, which for Cassandra seemed a little weird. She was as jumpy as a cat, and Noah knew just the thing to calm her nerves.

"How come the Wards ended up in Chicago? I thought all diamond-cutters were in New York?" he asked.

"We were there. Forty-seventh Street. Third generation. But about the time I turned fourteen, Dad wanted to move, so we did." She shrugged.

"Fourteen, huh? That's a hard time to start over. High school must've sucked for you."

"Yeah, but I managed," she said, turning up the volume on the remote.

Okay, change the subject Noah. "It suits you," he said.

"What?" she said, turning down the volume.

"Diamond-cutting. Elegant, sharp, but you can't look away."

Her head tilted to the side, a smile curving the corners of her mouth. "Maybe."

"Why do you do it?"

"Because it suits me," she said.

"What's the biggest diamond you've cut?"

"Four carats."

"Damn. Somebody really loved his wife."

She shook her head. "Nah. Not Mr. Sanderson. This was for his mistress. He needed the biggest rock in Chicago for her."

"Did Mrs. Sanderson ever find out?"

"Oh, sure. He came in two weeks later and Dad cut him a 4.1 carat ring for his wife. You see all kinds."

Then she went off, telling more stories, making him laugh, and scaring him more than a little bit when she talked about being robbed last summer. But nothing ever seemed to shake her. And why was that?

"I'm glad you have a good security system."

She laughed. "Although right now it's a pain in the butt. Power goes out. *Pbbtt.* Doors are locked. You're stuck. Can't get in or out."

"I don't think that'd be such a bad thing." Noah looked up at the ceiling, clearly considering the possibilities. "No, I think that could be a lot of fun."

Cassandra smiled. "Well, yeah, but Kimberly would disagree with you."

"Ah, Kimberly of the Counter."

"Yeah." They settled into a more relaxed silence. Eventually, his hand crept around her shoulder and she shot him a look, but didn't say anything. He'd never worked this hard for a woman before. Though he didn't want to dwell on it because there were too many reasons that this wasn't smart. When he turned her face toward him, her eyes met his and she smiled. It was all the invitation that he needed.

He started out slower than he'd done in the last twenty years, even slower than when he had Jessica Price just where he'd wanted her—in the back of his dad's old Ford.

Cassandra was no fifteen-year-old virgin. She was a living, breathing fantasy. Her lips were soft, pliable, giving, and he ached to deepen the kiss, but when this was all he had to look forward to, then he was determined to take his time. So he did.

He was very careful with his hands, although they were all too aware of the ripe flesh that was just within his reach. After the first kiss, she pulled back, acting like that was all there was. Noah smiled. "Don't tell me you think that's as good as it gets."

She laughed. "Right. So how long are you planning on making out on the couch?"

He shrugged. "Hours."

Her mouth opened, then closed. "Oh, come on. Why are you doing all this? We'll skip the perfunctories and can be hitting the sheets in my room."

She looked panicked and out of sorts, but he kept his hands on her and shook his head. "I can't believe that every man you have been out with is that much of a jerk, but okay, there you have it. Relax, sweetheart, all that's going to happen is a little kissing here."

She was still confused, he could see that in her eyes, but he liked it. He liked keeping her on her toes. There was a whole other world out there that she was missing, and he was going to be the one to show it to her.

He lowered his mouth again and filled her with his kiss. Tonight, he knew what he wanted. It took a while, almost two hours. Letterman was just signing off when he finally heard the first sound of success. He smiled against her mouth.

It was simple, and quiet, and nothing of note, but it was the first time that he'd heard her sigh.

"GOOD MORNING, Miss Atkins. You're looking lovely today."

Benedict O'Malley's secretary preened under all the attention. She was a nice lady, even if she probably was somebody's grandmother. "Mr. Barclay. Are you trying to charm your way into the transportation project?''

Noah settled himself into the metal chair across from her desk. "I don't think your boss can be bought. If he could, I don't want to be the one to tell city council. Is he in?''

She pointed a thumb at the door. "Go on in. He's doing the monthly reports and he hates that, always puts it off till the last minute," she said, her voice dropping to a confidential whisper. Noah thanked her and then walked into Benedict's office.

O'Malley was sitting behind his desk, with the look of a man who would rather be at the dentist. When he saw Noah, he smiled tightly. "Thank you for delivering a man from death by boredom.''

Noah forced a smile. "It's all right. I owe you lots anyway.''

Noah had met Benedict two days before the gala where he'd first met Cassandra. Noah didn't know much about the history between Benedict and Cassandra, other than it had been bad. Benedict had moved back to Chicago to be near Cassandra and so far, thank you, God, Cassandra had always shot him down.

Benedict shoved his papers aside. "This city has gone overboard on the bidding laws. Sorry about all the red tape. It seems like overkill to me.''

"Chicago has had some problems in the past.''

"Not under my watch," said Benedict, leaning back in his chair.

It was a fine balancing act every time Noah saw Benedict. He wasn't quite sure that he trusted the man, and the future of Noah's potential bid sat in Benedict's hands as the city's head of purchasing and development. He had avoided thinking of Benedict with Cassandra, but now the visuals were there, and it didn't sit well inside him. Jealousy was a humbling experience, and Noah never liked to feel humble.

"What do you know about Charlie Robertson?" asked Noah.

"Alderman. Seventh Ward. I've never met the man, so don't know."

"I heard McCann construction is giving him some heavy contributions. You think he'll fight my bid?"

"I haven't heard that one," said Benedict after hesitating, which was never a good sign.

"You'll give me a heads-up if he comes to see you?"

Benedict smiled easily. "Of course." Noah didn't trust him for a minute. "How're things going with Anvil?"

"Found my architect today and have two more interviews with some foremen. It's starting to take shape."

"Good. I'm looking forward to doing business

with you, Barclay. This Old Boys network grates on the nerves.''

Oh, yeah, right.

CASSANDRA MET MICKEY at Woodfield. Marshall Field's, Nordstrom, Lord & Taylor, plus the added bonus of alcohol.

''You missed it last night. You totally missed it. Gruzinov, Baryonic machos. Where do you even start to look? God, the man is a genius.''

Cassandra took another bite of cheesecake. ''Sounds like a snoozer to me.''

Mickey dug into the salsa. ''I twisted Dominic's arm, and he showed up at the end.''

''Dominic's the smart one, waiting until the end. If I had known that was allowed, I would have shown up at the end, too.'' No, she wouldn't. She had been exactly where she wanted to be last night—discovering the myriad pleasures of kissing with Noah Barclay. He had finally left her house at four in the morning. It had been a new experience—saying goodbye to a man with her clothes still intact. No man had ever waited for her before.

''Tell me about the dog,'' said Mickey, crunching happily.

''No rabies.''

''Where are you going to put him?''

"I'm not going to keep him, just setting him up until his owner claims him."

"That is just so weird. I can see J. with a dog. Maybe Beth with some cute puppy, but you? All that doggie hair on your clothes?"

"I don't let him touch me," Cassandra admitted.

Mickey laughed. "Well that explains it," she said and then changed the subject. "Jessica wants us to have a slumber party. She feels like she's losing a part of her old individuality since she's been married."

"She's been reading those books again, hasn't she?"

Mickey nodded. "It's a phase. It'll pass. You up for something? Maybe facials and desserts?"

Cassandra thought about it for a minute.

"I'm in," she said, because she was drifting apart from her friends and didn't like it. And she needed something to remind her about the parts of her life that she really loved.

Mickey took a sip of tonic water and then changed the subject. "So, what else is going on in your life? You took off early after the wedding. One moment you were breast-deep in men, the next you're gone. So who got lucky that night?"

Cassandra shrugged it off. "I wasn't feeling well."

Mickey dug in the bowels of the bowl for the chip crumbs. "Sorry about that, but I have something that will make you feel worse. Beth and Jessica want to get you married, or at least involved. When Beth gets back from the honeymoon, I predict much lectures on the joys of couplehood."

"No, I don't think so."

Mickey shrugged. "I've tried to stay impartial, you know, don't want to get involved, but I thought you could use the warning because it's not going to be pretty."

Cassandra was starting to believe that married people had acute myopia. "I'll be fine."

Mickey popped the last few bites in her mouth and grinned. "Although, Dominic's got some cop friends..."

"Leave it alone," said Cassandra, using her don't-mess-with-me voice, which always worked.

Mickey held up her hands. "Sorry. I forgot. I'm Switzerland."

Actually, Cassandra did feel a little different this time around, but she wasn't ready to spill her secret yet. Noah was her test. Maybe she could do the touchy-feeling kitsch, after all.

Her phone rang and she looked at the Caller ID. It was four-fifty. It was Benedict. His weekly call. She ignored it and didn't feel the usual surge of hostility. It seemed like progress.

Mickey nodded toward the phone. "You going to answer that? Or just make everyone in the restaurant annoyed at you because you won't answer your phone."

Cassandra held up her phone and powered it off. "Happy?"

"Happy."

After the bill was paid, Cassandra pulled the list from her purse. "What's that?" asked Mickey.

"I'm helping a girl at work discover her new self-image."

"So what items are required for a self-image do-over?"

"Knit pants, black. Poet's shirt, white, of course. American Woman Blush #357, Perla lipstick in Soft Mauve."

"You have the color number memorized?"

"Of course. Want me to help you, too?"

Mickey held up her fingers in a makeshift cross. "Back, back, I say!"

"Oh, come on, just the clothes. We'll find something new, and sexy, and Dominic can have a fine time."

When it came to Dominic, Mickey really was a sap. She pushed up her glasses and smiled. "Let's hit it."

4

THE BARCLAY ESTATE was a massive monument to capitalism, with hallways that echoed and wall-size landscapes in every room. Noah had always thought it was overdone, but it wasn't worth causing World War III, so he kept the thought to himself. Anyway, he had his own ideas for a home, and the Barclay estate wasn't it.

He was here to meet with his father, the larger-than-life Robert Barclay, who was also massive and overdone, but Noah kept that opinion to himself, too. Besides, how could you not love your dad, even massive and overdone as he was?

Noah liked being back in the States; now he felt like he was home. He had spent most of the post-college years on various continents building up his own company, Anvil International.

Anvil had been Noah's brainchild. There were opportunities overseas. Places in need of bridges and roads, and he was determined to build them. Noah had mixed his engineering degree with a worthless secondary degree in languages and actually began something both worthwhile and profitable. Noah had always been intrigued by the extraordinary. Mundane things quickly bored him. He needed the challenge, needed to keep his brain sharp. Now, he was thirty-four and ready to make his mark in Chicago.

He settled himself into the solarium and waited for his father to show up.

"There you are! Hiding out in here?"

"Only from Joan," Noah admitted. "I don't want to talk about a wedding. I don't want to hear endless descriptions of fabrics. The family would be much better off if she eloped."

His dad laughed and settled himself across from Noah. "She eloped once already. That's why we have to do this right this time, or so she keeps telling me. God willing, this is the last wedding we have to bear," he said, taking out a cigar from his pocket. Noah's mother hated Robert's cigars and would kill her husband when she found out.

"I thought you gave those up."

"Only a rumor, but don't tell your mother. So how's the bidding process? The *Herald* said they were cracking down and not letting any new companies on the list of potentials."

"I'll manage," Noah replied, thinking his life would be a lot less complicated if he could avoid

Cassandra until after his project bid was made. Anyway, it was worth the risk. She was worth the risk.

"What's put that smile on your face, son?"

Noah had worked through problems in the past. He would again. He leaned back in his chair. "It's summer, Dad. Isn't that reason enough?"

"You need to arrange dinner with Senator Jackson and Congressman Hastings. In fact, Sam's having a fund-raiser next weekend. You should go. You get those two to vouch for you and any bid you do will be snatched up in a second. I could help you."

Noah shook his head. "Thanks, but no. I want to be known for Anvil, not for being a Barclay."

"Stubborn."

"Independent."

"Chip off the old block." His father smiled, puffing happily. "Harry's taking Joan ring-shopping. You'll read about it in tomorrow's society page, I'm sure. She wants to hire a P.R. firm." Robert shook his cigar; the ashes fell into a fern.

"Harry's coming for dinner tonight. Talking caterers with her mother. You could stay."

"You just want someone to share the misery."

"Damn right, son. You're not going to keep an old man company?"

Noah smiled at his father. "Do I look like a sucker to you?"

Robert puffed happily at his cigar. "Nope. You're a Barclay. Through and through."

"I CAN'T WEAR THIS," Kimberly muttered.

"You put a camisole underneath it and it's perfectly acceptable, and it'll look beautiful with your skin."

Kimberly looked skeptical.

"Can we put it out for a trial run? I'll do the makeup and you can try on the outfit and I'll get Mark in the store. Then afterward, you can say, 'Cassandra, you are a genius, I will never argue with you again.'"

Kimberly still looked skeptical, but a part of her wanted to believe. Cassandra saw the hope in her eyes. Every woman wanted to believe.

"All right, but if it doesn't make a difference, I'm ditching it."

"Of course."

It did make a difference. Kimberly looked marvelous. It wasn't a full transformation, but the flowing shirt made her look soft and feminine, which for Kimberly was a good look.

"You can get Mark in here?"

Cassandra just smiled. Outside the crew was working as usual. No power outages today but Cassandra used her best walk. Sex and confidence all rolled into one shift of the hips. The entire crew turned and stared. Of course. Cassandra smiled.

"Mark, honey, can we talk for a minute? We're setting up our appointments for the next week and I'd appreciate it if I could get the schedule all worked out. Not that I don't have the most complete and utter faith in the fine job that you all are doing, but it just makes good business sense to cover all the bases. Follow me, please."

Mark followed. Of course.

Once they were inside the store, Cassandra took Kimberly into the back. "Now, if I had really thought this through, you'd have an earpiece, but this is improv. We'll manage fine. You look great. You're going to write down the work schedule for next week. Go distract him in the store and I'll duck behind the counter while he's not looking. Then I'll write down your instructions."

"You want me to distract him?"

"Honey, my plans for you include more than distracting him, but that's a place to start.

"Fluff your hair."

Kimberly obeyed.

Cassandra pushed her out the door. "Let's see what you can do."

Kimberly walked over to Mark, her steps more closely resembling a German goose-step than a seductive stride, but Mark wasn't watching. He was engrossed in a display of watches on the side wall. "You like those?" Kimberly asked.

"Out of my price range," replied Mark.

Cassandra rolled her eyes and then crept behind the counter. When Kimberly glanced around, Cassandra gave her the all-clear symbol and she moved back around the counter. "I need some paper."

Show him your wrist, wrote Cassandra.

Kimberly made a fine show of her wrists. "When are you going to be working next week? I mean, when are the crews going to be working next week?"

Cassandra angled to get a better look at Mark's body language. When she scooted a little to the right, she had a great shot of him from the waist down. So far, it was good. His hands were in his pockets, thumbs were pointing south. Male display stance.

Looking great. Use finger to hair.

Kimberly frowned, but twisted the ends of her hair, which had the added benefit of improving her posture.

Mark pressed forward against the glass. Cassandra smiled. Just like clockwork.

"We'll be out on Monday, Tuesday and Friday from eight to six."

"That must be a lot of hard work," said Kimberly, improvising, but it wasn't bad.

Try and touch his hand.

"Yeah. Mainly it's just hot."

"The heat is awful this year. Look at your hands!"

Cassandra smothered a giggle when Mark's hip jumped.

Bingo. Reel him in, honey. He's hooked.

Kimberly giggled a nice, throaty giggle, laced with nervousness. "You know, sometimes we go out after the store closes. Happy hour. You could come sometime. And any of the other guys that want to come, as well."

Mark leaned in closer. There were definite signs of life surging in his lower body region. Kimberly wouldn't have any trouble at all.

"Does Cassandra ever go?"

Cassandra frowned and Kimberly kicked her under the counter, which was so not fair, but Cassandra understood.

"Sometimes," said Kimberly, which was a good answer.

"Cool," said Mark.

"Cool," said Kimberly.

Then Mark's pelvis disappeared from the glass and Cassandra heard the door buzzer as he left.

She stood victorious. "Now you may say it."

"He might go to happy hour."

"Can you drink?" asked Cassandra, wanting to be parental, now that her baby was growing up in front of her eyes.

"I'm twenty-one."

"Good," answered Cassandra.

"I owe you one," said Kimberly.

Cassandra grinned. "I know."

ON TUESDAY, Noah found himself downtown once again. He'd had the last meeting with his foreman. That brought a smile to his face. His foreman. Things were shaping up at Anvil very nicely.

The El roared overhead as he entered her shop. The street shook beneath his feet. The electronic buzzer beeped as he opened the door and his smile got even wider just anticipating seeing her again. It'd been one week, which was a helluva long time for a man to wait. But the dreams kept coming at night. They bombarded him with more than he could handle. Seven days. Surely that would be long enough.

Right then she appeared and he realized that seven days wasn't nearly long enough.

She was dressed conservatively—for her. Tight blue jeans and a button-down that was unbuttoned one button too far.

Noah sucked in oxygen.

"Noah. This is getting to be a habit," she said, a snap in her voice, but her eyes looked pleased.

He had known quite a few women, skirted in and out of relationships. In his opinion, the idea that there was one person you were meant to be with was the product of some woman's overwrought imagination. But he had some connection with Cassandra. He felt it, not just in his glands, but in his mind, as well.

"I thought you might want lunch."

"No can do. I'm working solo today and I've got an appointment in an hour."

"You're a difficult woman," he said, wondering why he couldn't be interested in somebody a little less—difficult. And maybe that's all it was. Noah never trusted things that were too easy. In his experience, the best bridges, the ones that outlasted civilizations, were the ones that involved a lot of patience, a lot of work, and a hell of a lot of thinking.

She put a hand on the counter, her fingers stained with ink.

"I'm not difficult. I just have to do what I have to do."

"Do you have any appointments for the next thirty minutes?"

She shook her head.

Noah wasn't about to give up now. "It's warm, the wind's blowing off the lake. How about a walk? Just to the river and back. You could lock up. Put up one of those Be Back In An Hour signs. What could it hurt?"

He could see that she was tempted. She even took a step around the counter.

"A little walking can do wonders for the hips," he added.

"It takes a brave man to insult a woman's hips."

"That wasn't an insult." He reached out and palmed her hips, which were absolutely perfect, by the way. He drew her close. "A kiss can do wonders for the soul."

He brushed his lips across hers, nothing more than a soft kiss on a warm summer day.

She looked surprised when he drew back, and he was pleased at the disappointment he read in her face. Then he tucked her hand in his and smiled. "What do you need to blow this joint?"

"Let me get my keys," she said.

HE WATCHED HER as they walked, as she carefully studied the other jewelry stores they passed. She tucked her hands into her pockets, consequently pulling her jeans tighter. A couple of millimeters more and his blood pressure would be somewhere above eight hundred.

His fingers caught hers and pulled them free of her pockets. Health crisis averted.

They walked up Wabash and were surrounded by the oldest of Chicago's skyscrapers. For a man who lived to build, there was no better place in the world to be. The Sears Tower, the Hancock Building, the

Wrigley Building. Chicago was a city where the buildings towered far above the clouds.

He pointed them out as they passed, and he was surprised that she didn't know more. Hell, she had lived here for the past ten years, unlike him. "You don't get out here much, do you?" he asked.

"No."

They walked up to the Michigan Avenue Bridge and stared out over the river.

"You build bridges, don't you? I like that." The wind blew her hair around her face. Every now and then a car would honk, but he noticed that she didn't react at all. He was ready to hit somebody, but to her, they just didn't exist.

He shook off his anger and slowed his breathing. "A bridge isn't just a road. It's a technical marvel. You have to understand hydrodynamics, structures and support, geology and physics in order to make it work."

"Beth said you're trying to bid on the highway project."

"I've got a lot of hoops to jump through to get on the approved vendor list, but I'll make it."

"You're a Barclay."

"The Barclay name doesn't mean anything in the construction business. Yet."

"I've got friends in the Office of Purchasing and Development."

"O'Malley," he announced. He'd been waiting for her to bring him up. He watched her face closely for signs of some emotion, but she was carefully blank.

"I could help you out," she offered.

Noah tried to ignore the punch in his stomach. "You're still friends?"

She shaded her eyes against the sun. "No. But I could play nice. Get you a leg up."

He tilted her chin, but didn't like the way she was skirting his gaze. She wasn't a woman who normally avoided meeting his eyes. "No. I get there on my own. Understand?"

For a long time she studied him, then she began to smile. "I like your style, Noah Barclay."

"I get what I want."

"Spoiled?" she asked, one eyebrow arching nicely.

"Persuasive," he said, just to make sure she knew.

5

IT WAS A PERFECT day. Being with Noah, she could relax, lose the pretense. Let the rest of America's women worry about posture and games. Today she was just going to be herself.

A hot-dog vendor caught her eye and she smiled. It was nothing flirty, it was just because she was having her perfect day and she wanted the world to know.

And then he whistled.

She shouldn't have let it bother her, but it did. Cassandra shut her eyes and waited, started to count in her head. The guy's disapproval always came.

Noah kept quiet. His jaw was tight and his eyes looked dead ahead.

"Sorry," she said, mainly out of habit. Sometimes her moves were unconscious, sometimes they were premeditated, but this time she had just been happy.

"It's not your fault," he said, but her dates always said that. It was never her fault, but nobody ever believed it. Except Noah?

They walked back to her store and she turned to tilt her face toward the sun.

"So if you don't walk, how'd you get that tan?"

She began to breathe easier. This, she could handle. Assume the upper hand.

"Why do you think I have that big fence in my backyard?" she said, tilting her head back farther, which gave him a long area of throat and cleavage to admire.

"That really wasn't the image I wanted in my head right now. You walk around with a hard-on too long and people start to wonder."

"You getting ideas, Mr. Barclay?" she asked, liking it when all that easygoing charm turned on a dime. His eyes flashed for just a moment before his gaze raked over her in one long sweep. A shiver worked through her from breast to thigh and back again. She rolled a shoulder. Her shirt was suddenly too tight and her jeans not quite tight enough to relieve the pressure between her legs.

Then he smiled. The spell was broken and the temperature returned to normal. She used her keys to stop the store's alarm from sounding and they walked inside.

"Home sweet home," she said, walking to the back room and putting her bag away. Meanwhile she waited and hoped that he'd follow.

And, surprise, surprise, he did. Sometimes men were so predictable.

"Thank you for the company," he said, brushing

her hair back from her face. "It's been a long time since I've taken a walk on a beautiful day with a beautiful woman."

"You've got an effusive tongue, Mr. Barclay."

"Effusive? I prefer the term practical."

"Practical?"

"Oh, yeah." He pulled her closer. "In some cultures, the tongue is considered sacred."

His flirting was easy and nice, and always made her smile.

"Yeah, right. Which cultures?"

"Mine." He kissed her long, slow, deep. Her normally steely thigh muscles melted into nonsteely ooze. "It's for paying homage to the mouth."

Then he worked his way to her neck. "The ear."

The stubble of his jaw scraped against her neck and she giggled at the tickling sensation.

He lifted his head and his hand trailed down her neck to her shirt and made quick work of the next two buttons, which exposed her practical white, cotton bra. "You, Miss Ward, are a fraud," he admonished.

"Support is important," she said defensively, like she was some sort of virgin, and then bit her tongue as he pushed the cotton aside.

Slowly he tongued her nipple, sucking in hard until she was breathing in time with him. Just when she had braced herself against the counter, anticipating more, he buttoned her back up. Quickly she disposed of disappointment-face.

However, he, the cad, was not done. Oh, no. The long fingers trailed down to her jeans, undoing the button, unzipping the zipper. He smiled at the edge of the silky black panties peeking out. "Now there's my girl." Then he bent down in front of her and licked right over the curve of her stomach, paying close attention to her belly button, and then sliding the black silk aside and giving one quick flick just above the top of her curls.

Weakly she moaned.

Cassandra sent a fast prayer to the tongue god, but the tongue god was not cooperating today. Noah zipped up her zipper, buttoned her button, and planted a quick kiss on her lips.

"Come to dinner with me Sunday night."

"Yes," she whispered, not even hesitating. She was still breathless and more than a little overstimulated.

"Just wanted to give you something to think about," he said.

She blinked, backing up against the desk, and then watched him go. "I will," she promised, but he had already left.

HER TWO O'CLOCK appointment was Steve Amesworth, whom she had never met before, but who wanted to find a pink diamond for his wife. He was a rush of energy as he bustled into the store, but then stopped when he saw her. "You're Ward?"

"Cassandra Ward." She held out her hand. "My father and I run the store."

His smiling eyes were charming. "Oh, sorry, I was expecting some little old guy with a beard."

Cassandra laughed. "That'd be my father, and most of the other diamond-cutters in the country."

Mr. Amesworth leaned against the counter, his eyes leaving charming and entering awareness. "I have to say that I consider myself one of the luckier diamond buyers then."

Yeah, it was a line she'd heard before. Since she'd started working the counter their business had doubled. Her dad was thrilled.

Cassandra coughed. "You needed to find a diamond for your wife?"

"A friend recommended you. His wife said this was the place for great diamonds."

"And it is. What size stone were you considering?"

"Big, honey. Only big."

She took a deep breath. "Color?"

"Pink. Lola loves pink."

Pink was good. Pink was expensive. "If you'll excuse me, I'll be right back."

He caught her hand. God, she hated that. The man-given right to touch her.

"I could come back and help you. What do you say?" he asked.

Cassandra waited for her bitch mentality to flow over her, to give her the power to zap Mr. Steve Amesworth right back to the rock from whence he came.

She waited. His hot fingers locked around her wrist.

The power didn't flow. Nothing came to her tongue. Her eyes were losing their laser sharpness and he stood there, the master of the single entendre, waiting for her to either run away or peel off her clothes right there on the spot.

Damn it, damn it, damn it.

"Regulations," she muttered, and then ran to the back.

Slowly she worked to breathe, calming the panic inside her. It was nothing but a temporary aberration. For eighteen years she had worked, she had perfected, she had channeled the power over a man. She was not going to lose it all because of one short, albeit perfect, afternoon.

She played up her cleavage, pulled her hair free from the ponytail and fluffed it, and began the quiet mantra.

I am the Bitch.

I am the Bitch.

I am the Bitch.

When Cassandra was at her most lethal, no man could stand up to her.

Even now, she was feeling the force's return and she smiled in the mirror. Yes. It was the smile that had sunk a thousand Saturday Night Steves.

Cassandra pulled out the velvet-lined box from the safe, pouring the diamonds on the display tray, and then sauntered back to the front. Mr. Steve Amesworth was toast.

"Here they are," she said, smiling confidently. "Your wife will love one of these. I bet she's a woman of exquisite taste," she added with a wink.

She took a deep breath, feeling the power surge inside her. Steve no longer looked so predatory. She pulled her loupe from between her breasts. Okay, so it's a showy gesture, but it put the shell-shocked look in his eyes.

It was all about control.

She held up a stone in her hand. "This one is nice. It's got a crack, but if we cleave right here, we can whack that little problem right off. What sort of cut does Lola like? Emerald, pear or brilliant? With this stone, I'd recommend an emerald cut. It's expensive, but it'll be beautiful when I'm done with it."

She kept up her spiel and Steve kept his hands to himself.

Eventually, he went home to Lola, his wagging tail now tucked firmly between his legs where it belonged. Cassandra had guilted him into a three-carat rather than the two-carat, just because she could.

"Why, honey? I thought you were thinking big? Around here we call that one 'small.'"

After he left, the buzzer sang its annoying little song and Cassandra sat in her chair, preparing to work. She examined the stone, finding the grain line. She pulled out her India ink and carefully began to draw the lines of the cut. Lola's stone was going to be a masterpiece; she had known how she would cut it from the first time her father had brought it into the store.

After cleaving the stone, she set it on the dop and began to polish. It was a process that was repeated for each facet. Cassandra began to smile as she worked. She even whistled to herself as her confidence returned. No more Ms. Nice Guy. It was time for Noah to succumb, to understand exactly who was boss in this relationship.

And finally she would have him in her bed, those big hands exactly where they belonged. On her.

JESSICA SAYS: "M., you there?"

Mickey says: "Under duress, but yes."

Jessica says: "What did she say about the fix-up?"

Mickey says: "What do you think she said? No. Not just 'no,' but 'hell, no.' Not just 'hell, no,' but..."

Jessica says: "I get the picture. You can cease with the dramatics."

Mickey says: "That wasn't dramatics, she really said—"

Jessica interrupts: "I think something's up. I called her to meet me for lunch next Monday and she refused."

Mickey says: "Why don't you leave her alone for a while? I think she needs space. Beth's wedding hit her harder than I thought it would."

Jessica says: "How could you tell?"

Mickey says: "I can see below the lipstick, the eyeliner, the foundation. The pain was definitely there. Besides that, she got a dog."

Jessica gasps and says: "A dog?"

Mickey nods, remaining silent in a wise-woman way.

Jessica says: "You think it's Benedict that's causing the trauma?"

Mickey plugs numbers into her computer: "Survey says no."

Jessica says: "What's up? We'll grill her when we see her. She bought the whole slumber party thing?"

Mickey says: "Oh, you say that like it's some v. clever ruse, like we *know* you aren't dying to rediscover the premarried J-woman again."

Jessica says: "Do you ever worry about that? Feel like you're changing into someone else? Someone boring."

Mickey says: "No. Change is not necessary to make me boring."

Jessica says, because she feels Mickey needs perking up: "How's the honey?"

Mickey sighs extravagantly.

Jessica says: "Enjoy the honeymoon stage. He's going to want you to cook soon."

Mickey says: "Are you cooking yet?"

Jessica says: "Hell, no. I do the laundry, though."

Mickey says: "Dominic does ours."

Jessica says: "I hate you."

Mickey says: "Hee hee hee."

Jessica says: "I'm not giving up on Cassandra. I think she just needs to meet the right guy."

Mickey says: "Just leave me out of it. I want to live."

Jessica says, with an evil laugh: "If I go down, we all go down."

Mickey says: "Just what I need, kamikaze camaraderie."

"Cassandra, it's Jessica."

"Yes, ma'am. What is the purpose of your call? If it's lectures on the joys of marriage, I'm not at home."

Jessica sighed, although it could have been a muffled sneeze. "I'm planning a party. Just the girls. Sort of a massive dessert/makeup high-schooly sort of thing. Three weeks from Wednesday. Can you be there?"

"Let me check my calendar." Cassandra stared up into space. "You're in luck. I'm free."

"Cool. Ink me in. Now, on to point two. Adam has this friend. We're going to the Blues Festival."

"Enjoy yourself. You'll have a fine time."

"We want you to go."

"Gotta work."

"Your store closes at five."

"Inventory."

"Oh, come on. It won't be that bad. His name is Les, and he's great."

"I won't date a man named Les."

"He's a nice man."

"I can meet boring men on my own."

"I said nice."

"I know, *I* said boring."

"Look, just give him an hour. I think you'll really like him. But look, we can do this your way. We'll lie and say that you have to leave town. The red-eye."

"You can't decide on your soul mate in one hour."

Jessica gasped. "Listen to you. You said 'soul mate.' Girl, there is hope for you yet."

Cassandra sighed. "Can I say no?"

"No."

"Can I lie and invent some excuse?"

"I'll see right through it. We best friends have X-ray vision."

Something akin to loyalty tugged at her. Cassandra didn't like loyalty and she really didn't deserve to feel loyal to a man she'd known exactly eleven days. Six months and eleven days if you counted back to Beth's wedding when he shot her down in cold blood, which further supported her no-loyalty stance.

Cassandra closed her eyes. "I can't."

"You're having a hard time with all the weddings, aren't you? You know we'll always be there for you."

Cassandra grasped on like the lifeline that it was. "That's exactly it. God, you can read me so well."

Anything but explaining about Noah.

He confused her, scared her, and pleased her. Those didn't bother her, though. The worst of it was the need. She was starting to need him, and that didn't work for her. In eleven days he'd turned her entire life upside down. Now she was actually considering breaking her rules. She was losing her edge, losing the strength that she needed.

Nobody seemed to understand that Cassandra needed her strength most of all. She'd been weak once. In ninth grade, she'd been voted the girl most likely to do the football team simply because she was stacked, pretty and different.

Cassandra had fought the tide for two years. She'd fought like hell in New York, but when they moved to Chicago and it started up again—just like before— she stopped fighting. It wasn't fun, but she'd be damned if she let it happen again.

Never again.

She started to dig through her closet, mentally preparing for a date with Noah that was less than twenty-four hours away. She had to have something fun, and nothing in her closet was exotic enough, skimpy enough or mind-blowing enough. No, now it was time to go shopping, and Cassandra lived to shop.

NOAH WAS WAITING at the bar at Pravda when he first saw her. Dear God in heaven. There wasn't much of her he couldn't see. The skirt was tight, lace and short, with little flowers playing peek-a-boo. The top, or what there was of it, was just as bad, or bountiful, depending on the point of view. A line of white strings ran from her neck down to the top of the skirt, two lace pieces covering her nipples, or he thought they were covered. *Please,* let them be covered. It was enough to cause a man serious palpitations. All across the room he heard the rustle of ten thousand cocks springing to life. Including his. She walked toward him, her hips moving to some primal rhythm, and he held his breath as he waited for those strings to start swaying as well.

Then she was there, pressed against him, and instantly he put his arm around her. It was partially a protective gesture and partially because, dear God, the sight of so much flesh was blinding him. The man next to her angled his head, just checking to see if when she leaned down—

Noah gave her his seat and then stood behind her, arms on either side, shooting the gawker a like-hell look. "You did this on purpose, didn't you?" he growled in her ear. He held his breath as she turned in her seat. No. All clear.

"What?"

"The dress."

She smiled, but it didn't reach her eyes tonight. "This old thing?"

"Sweetheart, every man in this place, including some lesbians in the corner, are just waiting to see if those strings move."

She laughed a chest-expanding laugh. "It's a genuine Carlos Miele. Brazilian."

Why couldn't he have picked a woman who was obsessed with shoes rather than South American fashion? "We have company for dinner," he explained. "Alderman Robertson from the Seventh Ward."

This time she frowned. "You didn't mention that."

"Want me to call it off?" he asked, leaving the choice to her.

Her head tilted, but her body held still. "Not unless you want to."

For a long time he considered her. He considered the steel that was there in her eyes, he considered the heavy flesh that was there, out in the open, for anybody, including himself, who wanted to check it out. He thought he had made progress on her issues. Obviously not all of them.

He paused, ran a hand through his hair. "No, we're going to deal with this."

She rose from her seat, not a care in the world, and every neck in the room rose with her. "I think I'd like the steak. I feel like meat tonight."

There was a ripple of male approval that ran through the room. Noah just sighed.

NOAH HAD HIS DOUBTS about the possibilities of his business dinner with Charlie Robertson, but Cassandra seemed confident enough. If she wasn't going to worry, then he wouldn't, either.

There was a testy moment when Charlie shook hands with her. His bushy gray brows shot as high as they could go, yet Cassandra didn't flinch. She smiled her flirty smile, not quite as deadly as normal, and told him what a lovely tie he was wearing.

Immediately he blushed. Over dinner, she listened, content to stay in the background. But it was later, when they moved back to the bar, that she began to shine.

Two older women entered the room. They looked elegant in silver and diamonds. One, he recognized as Muzzy Von Meeter, Beth's mother, but he didn't know her companion. Charlie did. His gaze stayed on the woman and Noah gave up trying to steer the conversation to the list of bidders. He'd been hoping to close tonight, but it just wasn't meant to be.

"She's very pretty," said Cassandra.

"Who?" asked the Alderman.

"Mrs. Tyborn. I cut a stone for her last summer, right after her husband passed away. Wonderful taste in jewelry."

Charlie cleared his throat. "Yes."

"She likes you."

He swiveled his head, glared at Cassandra. "You're an impertinent miss."

She flashed him her smile and waved a hand. "No. Look at the way she's holding her hand against her throat. It's an open invitation."

Noah began to smile, too. This was a woman who could steal his heart.

"I don't believe that."

"No, it's true. Look, see that couple over there.

Look at her hand. And she's having a good time. And look, there goes the smile. See that."

"Those are young people."

Cassandra shook her head. "Charlie, do you mind if I call you Charlie? A woman like me knows a virile man when I see him. Don't try to tell me otherwise."

He blushed. "What should I do?"

"Put your hands in your pockets, low, and then rock your hips forward."

He stuffed his hands into his pockets, but he refused to move his hips.

Cassandra picked her battles well. "That's good enough. You need to meet her eyes."

He quickly met the woman's eyes and then looked away.

"No, do it again," Cassandra whispered, "only longer this time. Count to five if you have to."

He looked into Mrs. Tyborn's eyes and they widened, a flush covered her blush-colored cheeks. Noah watched in awe, and the last of his reservations left the building.

For six months he had ached to have her in his bed. The notorious Cassandra Ward, his own living, breathing pinup. From the beginning he'd seen her intelligence and her wit, but now he realized that the biggest part of her, her kindness, she kept tightly bound under white satin ropes and, well, not much else.

Noah smiled to himself. Now he was on to her and she didn't have a chance.

Cassandra gave Charlie a quick shove in the back. "Now go over there and be yourself. She's all yours."

He took a quick glance at Mrs. Tyborn and then shook Noah's hand. "You'll be hearing from me, young man."

Then he turned to Cassandra. "You're a very nice young woman. You need to wear something more appropriate, but I like you, just the same."

Then he walked over, hands in his pockets, and the courtship ritual had begun.

"WHAT AM I GOING TO DO with you?" Noah asked as he drove her home.

She considered the evening a great success, although the jury was out on whether she'd get what she was hoping for. "I've got some ideas."

"Why the dress?"

"It worked out okay."

"Only because you're good with men."

"Honey, I'm the best there is with men," she said while examining her nails.

"God deliver me from a confident woman."

"Does it bother you?"

"Yes."

She sighed and folded her arms across her chest.

"There you go. That's why I have my rules, Noah. It bothers every man."

"You're not exactly the innocent party. That... that—dress, and I use the term loosely, is illegal in the state of Utah and seventeen other states, as well. You do this on purpose."

"I do not. And you're one to talk. Always teasing me and then never following through."

"Hypocrite," he said, one hand playing in her hair.

He was always touching her. Always so innocently, yet always so...not. "What are you going to do? We can't keep this up forever."

The hand slipped away. She sighed, already missing it. "When I make love to you, it's only me."

"No," she said automatically. The words "make love" terrified her. Especially when "making love" involved Noah.

"Have you slept with anyone since the night of the wedding?"

"That's none of your business," she muttered.

"I'm not asking because I'm jealous. I'm asking because I want to know."

"No," she said quietly, because she had never been a liar.

"Why?"

"Because I haven't met anyone who's worth it, that's why," she said, shooting him a sideways look.

"Did you ever think that something is going on between us? Something more than just sex?"

He met her eyes and she willed herself to not look away. She felt herself falling deeper into the unknown. Too far, too fast. When it came to sex, it could never be fast enough, when it came to her heart, it just wasn't gonna happen.

So she licked her lips in one long, slow circle that she only saved for dire circumstances. "You make me hot, you make me wet, you make me wild. But that's all."

"You're not going to distract me."

She rolled down the car window and pressed her head back against the seat. "Could I distract you?"

"I'm not one of your minions, so don't even try it."

"Oh, come on, big guy," she said, her hand reaching out, finding the thick bulge in his pants. She savored the touch like a fine-tuned stick shift.

His jaw tightened, his fingers tensed on the wheel. Still she played. Eventually, she realized he wasn't playing back. Her hand returned to her lap.

"Why don't you admit it? How come it's so hard for you to commit?"

She laughed. "You think I have the commitment problem?"

He nodded. "Yeah, I do."

"I'm not here to talk about my problems. I'm not sure I even want to talk."

"Sure you do."

"I don't understand you."

"I'm not having this argument, not while you're wearing that dress."

"So you like my dress?" she purred. She knew from the moment she laid eyes on it—hanging alone in the back corner at Marshall Field's—that they belonged together.

"Oh, Cassandra. There isn't a man born who wouldn't adore that dress. Most men would just give their right nut to be sitting in this car with you. In fact, I'm sure I was getting a lot of death-threat thoughts back there because everybody else is alone in their shower, and I've got the real thing."

"You don't sound mad," she said cautiously. Usually, the alpha male displayed signs of temper when someone approached the female.

"Mad will get me nowhere. Patience will get me exactly where I want to be."

"Where's that?" she asked in her throaty, take-me-to-bed voice, happily recognizing that he wasn't mad.

He raised his eyebrow, not succumbing to throaty, nor "take-me-to-bed."

She slumped back in her seat. "Men don't resist me."

He had the absolute nerve to laugh. "Are you going to stamp your feet now?" he said. "Watch out, you might start falling out all over."

"I'm taped."

He shook his head and eyed her breasts. "That's just criminal. They don't put duct tape on the Mona Lisa."

She exhaled deeply, did so more out of habit than anything else. "The dress is for effect only. If you show too much, it's just embarrassing, sort of like ripping your pants. But if you make people wait, wondering if anything's going to happen, then that's what you're looking for."

She shouldn't be spilling her secrets to him, but she owed him something. A little bit of herself was due him because he wasn't mad and because, secretly, she liked him, which wasn't something she said about men. Ever. But she suspected he knew that.

"You analyze everything, don't you?"

"Of course."

He pulled up to the curb outside her house. Looking so handsome and privileged, she felt something bump inside her. Not between her thighs, but closer to her heart.

"Are you going to come inside?" she asked.

"Nope. Not coming near you," he said, then walked around and helped her out of the car. He

didn't quite hide the quick gasp when she bent over
to pick up her bag.

"Spoilsport," she said, stepping into the cool air.
He walked her to the door and she unlocked it. "One
kiss?" she asked, leaning back against the honey-oak
door, sliding one heel up the frame that she had
nearly killed Spawn for scratching. She rested
against him, not because it was part of her ritual, but
simply because she wanted to.

"One," he said.

He planted a kiss on her lips, took another long,
hard look at her breasts.

"You do have an all-over tan, don't you?"

"Come inside and I'll let you see," she whispered,
but she knew he wouldn't. He'd drawn his line in the
sand and he was waiting for her to cross it.

She kicked at the wooden porch with the toe of her
shoe. "So, if we have sex, I can't sleep with anybody
else?"

"We're not going to have sex, sweetheart. It's making love and you know it."

She gulped. Torn between the impressive thought
of him in her bed, finally, touching her, or sending
him off into the night, leaving her—alone. "And if I
agreed to that, what would happen?"

"You mean, right this moment or tomorrow?"

"I've got a good idea about the 'right this moment.'"

He laughed and shook his head. "Oh, no you don't. If you did, you would've given in a long time ago."

She eyed him. She liked his easy confidence. He reminded her of—her. "Sure of yourself, aren't you?"

"Not gonna let you chew me up like those choir-boys you must've known, if that's what you mean."

"Tell me about tomorrow."

At that moment, Spawn began to howl. "It sounds like you've got to feed the animal."

She nodded. "Will you wait?"

"For you, sweetheart, I'd wait forever."

He watched her go, moonlight dancing between the lace and the flesh, touching her in a way that no mortal man ever would. God help him, he was in love.

6

CASSANDRA KNEW the games were over. She was tired of trying to play mind-chess with him. At one time, she might have gotten a thrill from the whole thing, but now she just wanted to be held. By Noah.

Having sorted out Spawn, she returned to the living room and found him leaning against the couch, hands in his pockets, hips rocking forward.

Traditional mating posture. Her hand rose to her throat. "We need to talk first."

"I'm listening."

"Rule number one. No promises."

"Agreed," he said easily. Too easily.

"Rule number two. No exclusivity."

He shook his head. "Nope."

"Okay."

He raised his eyebrow. "Define 'okay.'"

She thought for a minute, not because she was really contemplating non-exclusivity, but because she needed him to think she was. She hadn't seen another man since before Beth's wedding; worse, she hadn't wanted to see another man. She wanted Noah, and no one else.

But deep inside her, she knew he wanted more from her than exclusivity. He wanted the part of her that she kept hidden from everyone. He wanted to hear her fears, her dreams, her vulnerabilities and her secrets.

He wanted more from her than just her body. He wanted her heart.

That was the thought that terrified her most, because she knew that this wasn't forever. Cassandra didn't do forever. Ever.

There he sat, his eyes patient and confident. Her very own Satan holding out the apple.

Finally, she nodded. "Deal."

He started to smile, which worried her more, so she quickly worked to regain order. "Rule number three. I do not dress up in costumes. No little girls, no cheerleaders, although I can do French maid if I'm feeling Continental."

"I don't like costumes."

"Also, we are coming to the subject of oral sex."

"Not a problem."

"You haven't heard my conditions."

He sat an inch closer and she could feel the heat emanating from him, already warming her. "I don't need to hear your conditions."

"Rule number four."

"How many of these do you have?"

"Five. Rule number four. I need a doctor's signature on your medical condition."

He reached into his pocket and pulled out a piece of paper. "I believe this will work for you."

"You had a physical?"

"I'm a gentleman. It seemed the right thing to do. Rule number five?"

"Condoms. Always. No exception."

"Agreed. Are you done now?"

"Yes, now we can begin."

"Just like that."

"Yes."

"You don't have a legal waiver I need to sign as well?"

"No." She stood up and lifted her hands to the buttons at the back of her neck, walking toward her bedroom.

He stopped her, pinning her against the back of the couch. "Wait a minute. Did you ever think I might have some conditions of my own?"

She shook her head.

"Rule number one. I get to undress you. My own pace, my own way." His fingers slid between the silk cords that kept her dress upright, back and forth, making her smile. This was familiar territory.

"How many rules do *you* have?" she asked, thinking this could be fun.

"I don't know. I'm making this up as I go along.

Let me think. Rule number two. Ah, yes. No rushing. I won't be rushed. It's going to take as long as it takes."

Weakly, she nodded. "Rule number three?"

"I think I'm going to kiss you now."

"Okay," she said, her voice starting to crack.

Noah lowered his head and she closed her eyes. Then he placed a soft kiss on her lips. She waited, and waited, and finally opened her eyes.

"I wanted you to see me," he said, cupping her face in his hands. "That's all." This time he kissed her for real, a slow, heart-pounding exploration of her mouth that spoke of the promises he had said he wouldn't give.

"Now we're going to talk about that dress."

She lifted her hands to the back of her neck. "The buttons are—"

He shut her up with a kiss. "Did I ask for your help? I don't think so." He pulled her hands behind her and placed them on the back of the couch. "There, you just stay here for a minute."

Heat pulsed through her, heat and a quivering excitement. He always did that to her, made her feel adored.

His mouth pressed to the base of her throat and then followed the path of the strings, stopping when he got to the top of her breast. She wiggled, her nipples stuck to the lace that at one point in time had been a good idea. Right now it was hell.

Ignoring her small moans of what she liked to think was protest, his tongue began to play, tangling over, under the strings, all the while searing her flesh. Her hands lifted to pull him even closer, but he was too fast and, without raising his head, he put them firmly back on the couch.

Still not satisfied, she took a step closer, until she could feel his erection pressing into her stomach. Come on, honey. Right there. She pushed her hips against him, rubbing up and down.

He stopped kissing her and raised his head. "No, no, no."

She glared.

He brushed a kiss on her forehead. "My way. You're too focused on getting to the other side, but, honey, tonight it's all about the bridge."

She was going to die before he built his bridge. She pressed her legs together. Tight. He noticed, of course, and pressed one strong thigh between hers. "We'll get to that later."

Then he bent his head again and laughed. "You know, I'm starting to love this dress." His mouth covered the lace flower that covered her nipple and sucked. Oh. God. She settled herself on his thigh. His mouth would suck, release, suck, release, and she began to sink lower. A warm haze wrapped around her, her vision graying, her lashes drifting shut.

When his mouth moved to the other breast, his fingers soothed the soft skin at her waist, up and down, soft, gentle, her blood pumping in time with the rhythm that he established.

Her hips ground against his hard thigh and she felt herself grow wet. She knew that his trousers would be damp from her, but he didn't seem to mind, and she was too turned on to stop.

Then he reached beneath the strings and carefully undid the tape that held her breasts to the dress, shaking his head. Next, he bent his head and kissed each tip, soothing, his tongue drawing the same slow rhythm that he used everywhere. He was going to kill her, and she still wasn't anywhere close to naked.

"Now," he said, and she held her breath. *Hallelujah*.

He bent and picked her up easily, and she curled an arm around his neck. "Which way?"

She smiled. At last. "Paradise is second door on the right."

He laid her down on the bed and she waited for him to start getting undressed. Instead, he placed a pillow beneath her head and a pillow underneath her hips.

"Now it's time to play," he whispered, and she

wondered what he considered all the other stuff. She was ready to ditch all that and dock this baby.

He spied the candle she kept next on her bedside table. Lavender, to soothe the senses. "Matches?"

"In the drawer."

She watched as he lit the candle, the glow from the flame illuminating his face. It was a picture that she was going to hold close in her heart. The shadow of stubble on his jaw, the fullness of his mouth. And his eyes. Dark, nearly black, and full of her.

His fingers went back to the strings at her neck and he traced up and down, this time all the way from neck to nipple, never actually touching her skin, just letting the silk cords do it for him. She squirmed a response to the heavy pounding between her thighs.

"You said the buttons were at the back?" he asked. He lifted his head, his eyes traced over her skin. She nodded and he lifted his hand, ready to undo the buttons, ready to free her from the torture, but then he shook his head. "Not yet."

She screamed.

He smiled. "Sweetheart, you're not the only one with rules." He adjusted the neckline of her dress until her exposed nipples were poking through the strings. "There. Remember. The dress was your idea. You wear it, you pay the price."

She shifted, but then realized when she moved the

silk rubbed against her breasts, abrading them even more.

He lowered himself farther down on the bed. His mouth explored the skin that showed through the cut-out at her waist. She lifted one knee, the skirt inching higher, and he laughed. *Laughed at her*. As if it was funny. "You've got such gorgeous legs, but you know that, don't you?"

He began at her ankle, holding it in his hands, pressing a kiss against her instep. "First we start low," he whispered, and then began to forge a path behind her calf to her knee.

He would kiss her skin, and just when she was ready for him to move an inch higher.... He'd stop. And talk. He told her how much he wanted her, told her how beautiful she was. One time he actually stopped and slid back up beside her, leaning on an elbow, and played with her breasts.

"Can we get on with this?" she asked, thinking if she didn't come soon, she was going to die here. Her neckline was spread-eagled across her breasts, like some ancient priestess at sacrifice.

"It's still early," he said.

"I have some things to do later on," she said, desperately needing to come. "Toys." Men loved her toys. They loved the idea of using them on her, and she knew exactly how to get to orgasm in three seconds flat.

He smiled that wicked smile, and she thought she had him. Then he shook his head. "No toys. You won't need them."

God, he didn't *know* what she needed, or he'd be inside her. Deep, deep inside her. Oh. She ground her hips. That was a mistake. Her body was crying here. Literally crying. Couldn't he see that?

"*I won't need them,*" she parroted. "I'm going to explode here. Soon. Do you understand that? Soon. I'm going to scream again, louder, and this time people will come running—this is a quiet neighborhood—and the police are going to want to know what's going on, and I'll tell them what's *not* going on."

He bent and kissed her lips. "I said I wasn't going to be rushed." Then he rolled her over onto her stomach and put the pillow back beneath her head. "If you need to scream, just use this. Nobody'll hear a thing."

She arched her butt in the air and screamed into the pillow.

7

IT WAS HUMILIATING, and Cassandra was glad there were no witnesses. She was moaning, pleading and aching. The proud-woman-conqueror of men was an amoebic mass of jelly. He was still somewhere around her waist, having moved exactly sixteen inches in the last hour. Sixteen freaking inches.

Noah's current target of leisure was the sweet spot just above the back of her knee. His hands would knead into her flesh, his mouth sucking there until she couldn't take any more, but he didn't give her much of a choice. He had raised the lace of her skirt, the bare flesh of her butt exposed, out there, and on fire.

"This is the prettiest set of cheeks. You don't mind, do you?" he asked as he drew his finger right between them.

Oh, God. He touched her everywhere, the back of the knee, the base of her spine, the top of her thigh. She would writhe in the sheets, grinding in a manner more reminiscent of a frenetic porn movie. She was pathetic, she was exposed, she was falling apart.

The man was killing her. She was going to die from lack of orgasm. There was a certain irony there, and tomorrow she would dwell on it.

She raised her head, just inches off the pillow, she had no energy for anything more. The pulse between her thighs pounding, hammering, pulling her inside out. "Please," she begged.

She couldn't see his smile, but she knew it was there. He slid one finger up the back of her thigh, to flirt at the top of the Y. She scooted lower, trying to plant herself right on that devilish finger, but he slid on top of her, covering her—oh, momma—and his hands, those large, capable hands, ran around and cupped her breasts.

It was better than the exposed teasing from a minute ago, but when she felt the thick bulge caressing her from behind the steel of his pants, she realized that she had jumped from the frying pan into the fire. She ground against him, and he held her tight, his hands kneading her breasts, his lips buried at her neck.

"How much longer?" she gasped, working against his erection, desperately trying to get off.

"Did you ever do this when you were a kid? Sure you were separated by a thin layer of clothes, but you could feel everything..."

"Yes, but now we're adults. We can do things

without the extra barrier of clothes. We could just rip those pants right off you."

Noah laughed against her neck. "Poor thing. You ready to get rid of that dress yet?"

"Oh, yes. Thank you, thank you, thank you."

His long fingers slipped to the buttons at the back of her neck and slid them free. Her hands slid underneath the damned strings to free herself, but he stopped her. "No."

He turned her around and pulled her up until she was facing him, sitting on her knees.

Slowly, he pulled the flimsy material down to her waist, and he stared, shaking his head.

Cassandra, who had never had a lack of self-confidence about her body, began to worry. "What?"

"No wonder I've had trouble sleeping. Now, the dreams are only going to get worse. You're going to ruin me for another ten years. At least."

"You've had trouble sleeping?" she asked, then gasped as his finger ran over her nipples and down to her stomach.

"Every night for the past six months."

His hands slipped beneath the lace of her hips and started to slide it down, lower and lower. She wiggled as the material shimmied down her thighs, and then she looked up at him, some part of her remembering her vampish training. "Can I take this off now?"

Before she realized what he was about, his finger slid between her thighs, one trip back and forth. It was just enough to fire a bolt of pleasure through her. She fell backward on the bed, her eyes drifted shut.

Then his hands slid the material the rest of the way off and he tossed it aside. "No, thanks. I've got it."

And there she was, naked on her own bed. Her body was more aroused than it'd ever been, her breasts full and aching, and a sheen of sweat covering her skin. He didn't touch her, his heated gaze moving from her head to her toes, settling on her breasts, her belly, the wet curls between her thighs.

She propped up on one elbow, letting her hair fall over her face. She slid one foot up the other leg, making a very nice triangle that was angled toward him, visual indication of mating intent, as if the dampness on her thighs really wasn't a big enough clue. "So, what sadistic pleasure are you anticipating now?"

She was hoping against hope that he was through playing, because she really needed to ease the ache inside her.

He lay back, considering her. Finally, he nodded. "I think it's time."

She fell back. Oh, thank God. With smoky eyes she waited for him to undress, waited to see just exactly how he looked without clothes. She had extremely high hopes, and there was no disguising his size or the, uh-hum, breadth.

He put a pillow back under her hips and parted her legs. "Now, we're ready for step four."

Four? "Uh, Noah, how many steps do we have here?"

He smiled and looked at her. "Twelve."

She shot back up. "Twelve!"

"Well, yes. How many are you used to?"

"One. One. One. One."

He started to laugh, low, deep, and then, yes, he did shrug out of his shirt. Greedily she looked over the magnificent flesh. Oh, he was a beautiful animal, and tonight he was hers. "I'm not waiting another eight steps," she insisted.

He laughed, and pushed her back down, but she wasn't done making her point. "I won't. This is cruel and unusual—"

His finger slipped inside her.

"—punishment." She sighed, which took the sting right out of it.

He leaned over her, his broad chest flat on her breasts, and she was delighted to see he had a light coating of chest hair, just enough to tickle. He kissed her lightly at first, then more seriously, until her eyes were too heavy to stay open. "There you are. Keep your eyes closed. Relax, Cassandra. We've got all night."

Slowly, Cassandra relaxed, adjusting to the feel of his finger inside her, moving patiently, gliding back and forth. Just when she was starting to find her rhythm, the finger disappeared. Her eyes flew open. "What happened to Step Four? I liked Step Four."

His fingers drifted over her eyes, forcing them closed. Then she felt his hands. They were hot at her waist. "That wasn't step four, this is step four."

Then he put his mouth on her and she came apart.

Cassandra had considered herself a master at the art of oral sex. She had perfected going down on a man. She knew what was what, knew what to touch when, knew just when to adjust the pressure, knew exactly when a man was ready to blow. She was a connoisseur of pleasure, but right at this moment, she bowed to the master.

Oh, God.

His tongue would glide over her, not too hard, not too soft, pausing to blow or suckle just when she felt herself falling over the edge. And she came to the humbling conclusion that she was a mere novice at the art of love.

Each time she pushed herself higher, he would back off and then return, the pressure easing, but then it would return in intensifying force. Slowly, but surely, she was being cooked, right from between her thighs.

At some point, the room began to swirl into a rainbow of colors and her vision began to blur. She gave up trying to think, and instead, just followed the waves that crashed over her.

Weakly her hand grabbed a bedrail, needing something to hold on to as the world shifted around her.

She heard herself moan, and beg, and gasp, and scream. It was as if she had moved outside her body, because there wasn't enough room inside there for both her and her orgasms.

Sometime later, he let up, sliding next to her, stroking her hair. She rested her head on his chest and listened to the pounding of his heart.

"Noah, what's step five?" she whispered.

He smiled. "Sweetheart, I'm not done with four yet." And then he went back to work.

Cassandra was too weak to argue.

IT WAS NEARLY THREE o'clock in the morning when they made it past eleven steps. She had given up fighting, given up everything. She had never been so thoroughly loved.

Loved. At some level, she understood that. What he was doing to her didn't involve sex, it was going far deeper than the usual. If she had been able to think more clearly, she would have been scared. In fact, she knew that in the morning she was going to be terrified, but at this moment she was incapable of all thought. He had taken away her mind.

Quietly, he stripped off his clothes. Finally. She couldn't do anything, but sigh in bliss when he curled against her and she felt the hot brand of his flesh. He burned like a furnace, warming her, his skin touching hers everywhere. His hands roamed over her back, her breasts, her rear, and slowly he pulled her thighs apart.

She lifted her head, needing to make sure he was protected, needing to make sure she was protected. He stilled her with a kiss, whispering, "I've got it covered." Then she relaxed and gave herself up to his kiss.

Then he was inside her, and she worked to accommodate him, afraid that he'd overdone everything else and that she wouldn't be able to get into the best part.

Of course she was wrong.

He moved slow, at first. His hands stroked her, kissing her all the while. "You have no idea what you do to me," he whispered again into her ear. "No idea how I've dreamed of this since I first saw you."

She grasped his back, her fingers digging in tight. His hips began to move faster, his thrusts going deeper inside her. The sting of tears pricked at the corners of her eyes, and she blamed it on exhaustion,

PMS, anything but the man who was currently robbing her of her heart.

It was all that he said, but the words didn't matter. He kissed her, and loved her well, and then he held her close.

Eventually the moon fell, the sun rising high in the sky, a blanket of fire burning all that it touched. The sheet had long since disappeared and Cassandra buried her head against his chest, the rhythm of his heart lulling her to sleep.

NOAH HELD HER CLOSE, not able to sleep while she was in his arms. He needed to touch her, needed to plunder. He smiled to himself, wondering if she had plans for this evening. He had a few ideas.

She stirred, and he guarded her jealously, letting her sleep. He had used every dirty trick in the book last night to keep her from analyzing things too carefully, to keep her from freezing him out of her mind, and he thought it just might have worked. So he wasn't that rusty, after all.

He was actually feeling pleased with himself when her lashes lifted and he found himself staring into brown eyes that were nothing but softness. Heaven. He bent his head, ready to kiss her good-morning, when the soft brown eyes went wide with horror and she gasped, pulling the sheet over her head.

8

GOD, DELIVER HIM from the workings of the female mind. Noah took a deep breath and then peeked under the sheet. "Cassandra? Honey? Is there a problem here?" he asked, his voice calm and soothing.

"You need to close your eyes," she said, still under the sheet.

"I've seen you without clothes. It's nothing you need to get shy about. You exposed all but about five strategic square inches of that body to most of Chicago last night. I don't know why you're shy about it now."

"It's not that," she muttered.

He poked his head under the sheet. "Then what is it?"

She squeaked and pulled the sheet tighter.

"You can't breathe, sweetheart. Tell me what's wrong."

"No."

"Cassandra," he repeated, using a firmer voice.

"No. You need to leave. I never let men stay overnight."

"That wasn't in your rules."

"It's not usually a problem."

"Okay, I stayed. That's not a bad thing, it's a good thing. If it makes you feel any better, I've got a meeting at the office in sixty-five minutes."

He made a move to pull her close and she pounded her fist on his chest. "Don't."

Noah sat up and sighed. "Okay, stay under the sheet, but at least tell me what this is about."

"Give me just a minute," she said, and jumped out of bed, her face in her hands, and shot into the bathroom.

Noah smiled. Obviously their intimacy was getting to her. He waited, put his hands behind his head and leaned back. She just needed a little alone time. Understandable.

Five minutes turned into ten, which turned into twenty. He could hear her humming in the bathroom, but she wasn't taking a shower.

He pulled on his boxers, prepared to investigate, but then she returned, framing herself in the doorway. The sun slid over her curves. Her face. She smiled.

For a second, he forgot to breathe.

Then he noticed the smooth complexion, the glossy lips, the Mona Lisa smile—his first clue that Ms. Hyde had returned. "Why the sheet?"

"Your meeting is in exactly forty-five minutes and

I need to feed the dog. According to my math, that gives us about seventeen minutes. Do you really want to waste all that time talking?"

Oh, she was good. The voice was low and sultry. Her eyes were full of promise, and she even had Noah checking the clock, but he wasn't about to be swayed. "Why the sheet?"

She sauntered forward, her hips mesmerizing, it was a fatal combination for an ordinary man, but Noah was having none of it. He shook his head. "Why the sheet?"

She came and stood in front of him, tiny when she wasn't wearing her usual three-inch heels. Slowly, she drew her finger down his chest, her hands settled at the top of his boxers where his hard-on was just starting to make itself known. He grabbed the hand before it could explore further.

"You're not going to say anything?"

She shook her head, her hair fell in a calculated fashion over her breasts. Noah glanced over at the clock. They could get a lot done in seventeen minutes. Her eyes flashed with victory.

And he'd blow everything he'd worked so hard— hard being the optimal word—on last night. He gave her a kiss and picked up his shirt and pants, shrugging into his clothes.

"I'll talk to you tonight. Pick you up at seven? We'll get something to eat."

Quickly, he turned away, before the sight of all her flesh could shanghai him again.

CASSANDRA SLUMPED against the wall. Well, hell. She had been so sure she had him. She pulled on a robe and went outside to feed Spawn, who growled and watched her carefully as she approached.

"Yeah, yeah. Good morning to you, too."

The dog ambled over to the bowl of water and lapped it up. Cassandra shook her head. She needed to print up some flyers to put up in her neighborhood. No way was she getting stuck with the dog.

Spawn lifted his massive head and glared.

Cassandra shrugged and then began to smile. She'd only had a minimal amount of sleep, and her body felt like a wishbone, but it was going to be a glorious day. Spawn barked then turned his attention to his food.

By the time that Cassandra had done her morning exercise routine, she had time to ponder the full ramifications of last evening. In strenuous detail, she played over each and every touch, until she was getting herself worked up just from the memory. Noah Barclay was good. She'd seen the look in his eyes this morning, knew that he was thinking he'd gotten the best of her. Right. Like that was possible. Although he'd almost caught her without her makeup. Not in this lifetime.

She was going to have to be tougher. But if he did that step seven again, she might rethink her position.

There was a pounding at her door and Cassandra tied her robe tight and went to answer it.

It was Jessica. With the paper.

"What the hell is the meaning of this?" Jessica asked.

Cassandra picked up the *Herald* and glanced over it. "It looks like partly cloud skies, a high of sixty-seven degrees, and a chance of rain by Thursday. I can't help you, Jess. Weather is beyond my powers."

Jessica stabbed a finger at the column above it. "Here."

Cassandra read the mention of the Rotary Club's next benefit luncheon, and then right underneath, the mention of Noah Barclay. Last night. And her dress.

She immediately swallowed her panic. This was nothing new. She stared at Jessica. "And your point is?"

"Noah."

"What about him?"

"This was the reason you turned down the date, wasn't it?"

"I do not get fixed-up."

"Don't try and change the subject. You're dating him."

"Darling, I am always dating someone."

"Not seriously."

Instantly, Cassandra was serious. "I'm still not dating anyone seriously. Not even Noah."

That shut Jessica up. "Really?" she finally asked.

"Of course. It's just fun, nothing more," she said, her mind zooming over details of last night that were deadly serious.

Jessica patted her on the hand. "Oh, honey, you keep saying that if it makes you feel better, but you're lying your ass off. Look at that goofy smile. You're exclusive. You want a little time alone before we go through the interrogation, I can understand that. I like him."

"He's just a man," said Cassandra, fighting to keep that goofy smile off her face. Oh, God, but what a man.

BENEDICT O' MALLEY was at the downtown offices of Anvil International before 10:00 a.m. Noah was on his eighth cup of coffee, trying to concentrate on the budgets he'd gotten from the latest Asian project. Slowly he rubbed his eyes. What had he been thinking? He wasn't eighteen anymore. Those all-nighters could give a man of his age a heart attack, but what a way to go.

"Mr. O'Malley is here to see you," interrupted his personal assistant.

Noah stood as Benedict entered the office and held out his hand. "Benedict, always happy to see you."

Benedict ignored the hand and sank into the chair opposite the desk.

"I saw the paper."

Noah frowned. "You've got a step on me here. What paper?"

"Last night," answered Benedict.

Noah froze. There was no way that last night had made the papers. Considering his superhuman patience, it should have, but...

Benedict slapped the copy of the *Herald* down in front of him, and Noah looked at the small column in the Tempo section.

Cassandra Ward wowed the crowds at Pravda last night, on the arm of newly returned Barclay heir, Noah Barclay. Dressed—or not—in a design of Carlos Miele's, she turned heads and caused temperatures in the room to rise as we all wanted to know, exactly what was she wearing under the dress? This reporter thinks the always outrageous Miss Ward was au naturel. Only Mr. Barclay knows for sure and I'm not sure he's telling.

Okay, it was bad, but it could have been worse.
"Noah, I haven't known you for very long, but I

respect what you're trying to do, and building up a business can be hard on a man, but Cassandra? What are you thinking? She can ruin a man's chances in the community."

And it got worse. Noah had known this day would come, he had just hoped it wouldn't come this soon. "Spit it out, O'Malley. Your issues with her are completely personal, don't bring business into it."

"Stay away from her, Noah."

"Because you want her back?"

"Yes." Benedict settled his arms across his chest.

"I'm in love with her."

"Line up. Every man she blows falls in love with her."

Noah shot across the desk, then noticed Benedict's complacent smile, and forced himself to back down. Noah was being played on purpose. He took a pen in his hands, which was less satisfying than Benedict's thick neck, but it was all he had. "For a man who wants her back, you sure have a damned poor opinion of her."

Benedict's smile turned feral and added fire to Noah's rage. "You have to understand a woman like Cassandra. Fidelity isn't in her makeup. She needs male attention like a shark needs blood."

Noah closed his eyes. He knew what Benedict was doing, he just needed to think. "Go back to work. You're underestimating her."

Benedict stood and shook his head. "You think you can change her. She'll fall in love, you put a ring on her finger, and she'll swear her undying devotion. I was there, man. I was right in those shoes. But the ring didn't change a thing. As soon as some other bastard picked up her scent, she was there with him. I found them, Noah."

It was a story that Cassandra had never volunteered, but Noah willed himself to believe in her. Even while images of her and Benedict flashed in his brain. "That was a long time ago," he said, as much to himself as to the man before him.

"Consider yourself warned."

"About Cassandra?"

"Yes."

"You're going to torpedo me on the contract, aren't you?"

Benedict looked him straight in the eye. "No, why should I?"

Noah closed his eyes after Benedict left. He hoped to hell that Cassandra was worth $27.3 million because he had a strong feeling that that's what it was going to cost him.

NOAH TOOK HER to the fund-raiser for Congressman Hastings. This time he'd given her fair warning about the occasion and she'd chosen something more appropriate, yet still stylish because she wasn't dead. He kissed her when he picked her up, but it lacked the verve he'd had the night before. Something was wrong, so Cassandra did everything in her power to help.

"Okay, so tell me who're the ones you need in your pocket," she whispered.

"Cassandra, I'm not going to put anyone in my pocket. I'm just here to make sure that everyone sees me as a viable businessman in the area."

She nodded. "Okay. Why don't we start with Barbara Emerson, then?"

Noah looked at her, confused. "Why?"

"She's the power broker in the room. Look at the way Congressman Hastings has his head angled toward her. Attentive, but deferential."

"That's because she's a lady and he's a gentleman."

Cassandra patted him gently on the arm, humoring the poor dear. "No. Look. He's stroking his chin. Consideration and evaluation. She's telling him something and he's thinking about it. And look! Palms up, hands out. Openness." It was textbook. She was surprised he couldn't see it.

"He's a politician. He just wants to seem interested."

"Nobody is that good of a faker, Noah. Trust me. Now there goes the congressman. She's alone. This is our chance." She tugged at his arm.

Mrs. Emerson was a third-generation Emerson, with the diamonds of a fourth-generation Rockefeller. Cassandra eyed the diamond choker around her neck. That one was a fake, though. A good one, probably expensive enough in its own right, but zirconia nonetheless. The woman's makeup could use a little help, too. She'd been way too aggressive with the blush and the lip color was all wrong. Fashion sense got a high B. The blue, high-waisted design was perfect for her. Her outfit was slimming, elegant, and even accentuated the exact color of her eyes.

"Lovely dress," cooed Cassandra as she greeted her. "Where did you get it? Actually, no, don't tell me. You probably want to keep your designer a secret. I would, if I were you."

Mrs. Emerson laughed. "Miss Ward. I didn't know your interests ran to politics."

Cassandra felt the piercing blue gaze, and her first instinct was reinforced arm-cross; however, she was strong, and instead locked her hands behind her back in a traditional superiority/confidence gesture. Noah tucked his hands into his pockets, his body angled toward Cassandra. Male mating ritual. Her eyes flashed him a message, "Not the time." He ignored her.

Cassandra carried on. "Are you campaigning for the congressman?"

"Oh, you know me. I don't back anyone."

"Except for Alderman Brown?"

Mrs. Emerson cocked her head. "Why do you say that?"

"It's obvious you agree with his message—cleaning up the city, bringing back the values that were here before the days of corruption hit us hard."

Barbara's pupils dilated nicely. Bingo. "This council hasn't been tough enough," she said, and then she lifted her glass to Noah. "You're new back in Chicago, aren't you, Mr. Barclay? I'm a friend of your father's."

Noah smiled. "This is my home. I've been away too long. That's why I want to bid on the highway construction project."

Barbara stroked the skin above her throat. The tramp. Cassandra kept the judgment out of her eyes, but she did have to look away in order to pull it off.

Noah, typical oblivious man, didn't notice. "But I'm not here to talk business. It was just an opportunity to get acquainted, match some faces with the names, and see how the city has changed."

"Why don't you come to my house for dinner next month? And you, too, Miss Ward. I'm having a small reception for the congressman, and I think you'd fit in nicely."

This was it, this was it, this was it. Cassandra squeezed Noah's arm. "Thank you, I'd—we'd love to."

The rest of the night was a smashing success. Alderwoman Watson was fiddling with her straw until Noah drew her out. After that, her feet compassed in his direction and she offered to set up a meeting. Congressman Matheson's wife had overdone it on the martinis and was shamelessly mimicking Congressman Hastings, who was trying his best to escape, pulling at his collar, his eye casting around everywhere but at the woman in front of him. Cassandra took pity on the poor man and engaged the woman in a conversation about diamonds—a guaranteed female crowd-pleaser.

It was finally time to leave. Cassandra looked over the room and almost everyone was engaged in their own conversations. Fascinating. She was just about to leave when a pair of hands settled on her shoulders. Unfamiliar hands. She turned and stared into the dilated pupils of Judge Roscoe Warren. Trouble.

His dilated pupils fixated downward until they were stuck at her breasts, which were completely covered up and just not out there for public consumption tonight. Cassandra was torn. Here was her chance to practice new non-flirting techniques and be the poster child for proprietary, or...she could cause trouble.

"You should have worn your other dress tonight. A woman with a body like yours..."

It was no contest. She licked her lips and flicked a

button open, and then angled toward him. "A virile stud like you, more potent than champagne. Meet me in the coat closet," she said, pursing her lips together.

Judge Warren leered and staggered off into the direction she sent him just like a good little wanker. Men were really so gullible.

She ran into Congressman Hastings just around the corner, and began to chew on her fingernail, looking anxiously at various hallways of the reception area. "Something wrong, Miss Ward?"

"Congressman. I can't believe this. Silly me. Do you know where the coats are kept? I told Noah that I'd get my jacket, but I've had such a good time tonight, I've forgotten, and I really don't want to tell him that. He'd never let me hear the end of it."

Congressman Hastings nodded. "What were you wearing?"

"A light blue sweater."

"I'll get it for you," he said.

"Oh, you are such a gentleman," she said, and sat back and waited. It didn't take long. In thirty seconds Judge Warren emerged from the coat closet, his face flushed and his trousers unbuttoned, and Congressman Hastings emerged right after him, his eyes narrowed to pinpoints.

Cassandra plucked her sweater from the congressman's hand. "Are you all right? The old goat. You can never tell, can you?" she asked, staring balefully at Judge Warren. "He seemed like such a nice man."

"I'M SORRY about the paper," she murmured quietly on the drive back home.

Noah stretched an arm across the seat and squeezed her shoulder. "It's all right."

"You've been quiet."

"It was a long day."

He watched as she faked a yawn. "Yeah, don't I know it. Mr. Liepshutz's coming by the store tomorrow and I have a ton of things to do."

"Did you set up Judge Warren?"

She turned, wide-eyed and pursed lips. It was a look he was beginning to recognize.

"No."

He glowered at her.

"Maybe," she murmured, staring at her feet. Then she lifted her head. "But he deserved it."

"You don't have it easy, do you?"

She moved his hand. "Don't feel sorry for me. I don't like it, I don't deserve it. Do you know how pathetic it sounds? Oh, woe is me! Guys love me, girls hate me. Yeah, life sucks."

"That doesn't mean it's not a problem."

"A problem to be fixed, Oh, Mighty Bridge Builder? You're right. I could gain fifty pounds and no man would look at me twice."

"I would," he said, because it was the truth.

After they made it to her house, he walked her to the door.

"You're tired. I'm tired. Let's call it a night, Noah."

He didn't like to leave her like that, her eyes so lonely, but he wasn't going to chase after her too hard, either. "I've got something for you," he said, and popped his trunk, lifting out the heavy bag.

She stared. "Is this a dead body?"

"It's dog food. Spawn has got to be getting tired of the rice cakes."

She lifted a shoulder. "He likes the chips. You're going to turn Spawn into Spud with that much food."

He plopped the bag on her porch.

"All right," she agreed. "Bring it in, then, because I'm not the one with all the muscles."

He watched while she put out a bowl for Spawn. Then he drew her to him, stroking her soft hair, his hands massaging hers. "I have a call in a couple of hours."

"Who does business at 2:00 a.m.?"

"It's always the afternoon somewhere in the world."

"Oh, yeah."

"So, I'm going to leave you alone, even though it's tough."

She smiled up at him. "You're just being nice, but I like it."

He pressed her up against the wall, because she expected it. "Now do you believe me?" he asked, grinding his erection against her.

"Oh, my. You're going to let all that go to waste?" she asked.

"You've got circles under your eyes..." he started, and she pushed back against him.

"I do not!"

Then she tore off for the bathroom and returned in a couple of seconds, pointing to her eye. "There are no circles. This is Perla Studio Finish concentrated concealer in NC30, designed for long wear and invisible coverage, enriched with antioxidants. *There are no circles.*"

She wasn't making this easy. Contrary to what everyone seemed to think, nothing with Cassandra was easy. "Did I say circles? I didn't see any circles. Get some sleep. I've got big plans for tomorrow night."

She arched a brow, effectively diverted from the circles. "Oh?"

"You're going to need it."

"Does this involve step seven?" she asked.

He couldn't help but smile, but he filed the information away. Step seven was a winner. "It'll be my surprise."

Then he kissed her. Once, twice, then again because she had the most kissable mouth in the world. "You're tempting me," he said, trying to sound stern.

"Go home," she said, pushing him out the door.

He took one last look, *Beauty Framed In A Doorway*, and sighed.

9

THE NEXT MORNING, Noah had a meeting with Anvil's architect at his office. He'd found his foreman and his crews, now all that was left was to finalize the plans for the bid for the upcoming transportation contracts. Two weeks to deadline day.

It seemed fitting that just as all the pieces were falling into place with his latest project, someone—Benedict—felt the need to clear the air.

The e-mail was straight and to the point. Sure, it read completely professionally to a naive eye. But Noah had never been naive, though he could still handle this without blowing either the deal or his temper.

Benedict looked up when Noah walked into the man's office. He immediately frowned and Noah knew this wasn't going to take very long.

"I need to find out exactly what you expect on the financials. I've got Schedule N from the last few years, but because the work's been done outside the U.S., I didn't file a 943B."

O'Malley lifted up his hands in what should have

been a helpless gesture. "These are the rules, Barclay. I can't just bend them because you don't do it."

Noah had never been a big believer in rules. They just got in the way of what you wanted. So this was the way of it; he could walk away from the deal, walk away from his first, best chance to make a mark in this city. In his hometown.

No.

"Why even pretend? I'm the only bidder who's going to have an issue with this, aren't I?"

"Getting a little paranoid?"

"I would be less paranoid if you hadn't added this just yesterday."

Benedict shrugged. "Sorry. It's protocol."

Noah took a deep breath of calming oxygen to offset his anger. "Losing it" wouldn't do any good here. "Okay."

It did all sorts of painful things to his insides, but he could file a 943B in arrears with the IRS. It wouldn't mean a thing to the tax office, but O'Malley would have his blessed checkmark.

"I would say it's been a pleasure, but I'll pass," said Noah, and then he turned to go.

"Oh, Noah. Give my best to Cassandra."

THE WEEK PASSED quietly for Cassandra. She had only seen Noah once, and something was on his mind, but he wasn't talking. As a woman who believed that words were not the best way to communicate, she understood and left him alone.

He had told her that he would pick her up on Friday, just as she was closing, and five minutes prior he was there. Gotta like a man who keeps his promises.

"We're going shopping."

Cassandra took a step back and stared wide-eyed. "You shop?" *Wow, it was true. This man had no flaws.*

"No, but I'm making an exception."

Cassandra laughed. Yeah, she knew he had been too good to be true. "Why?"

"Because you're going to need a dress."

She sniffed, but was intrigued by the possibility. "I have a closet full of dresses. I don't need another one," she said, simply because she was a proud woman of impeccable taste.

Noah opened the car door and loaded her inside. "Trust me."

They hit a boutique on Michigan Avenue that she didn't even know existed. Of course, the clothes were more conservative than her normal style. As soon as she walked through the door, she shuddered. "I'm not wearing anything like this. It's not me."

Noah shot an apologetic glance at the saleslady. "Can we just try this?"

"Fine."

She knew she wasn't going to like anything, it wasn't going to look right, but she was willing to follow this through, just so he could learn his lesson.

Unfortunately, Noah was marvelous. He picked out a pale pink gown with a shallow bodice that hugged her down to the knees until it billowed out into a nice little poof. It looked so innocent on the hanger, but when she tried it on, complete with the little matching sandals—okay, it was her very own Cinderella moment.

When she came out of the dressing room there was a gleam in his eyes that warmed her all over.

"Looks perfect," he said. "You'll need to wear it."

She gave him the once-over, noting the casual khakis and shirt that he was wearing. "I think I'll be a little overdressed."

"Nah. Give me a minute."

And yes, he returned ten minutes later in a tux. She grasped a handy chair back for support, her knees not quite so steady. Maybe it was the element of surprise, maybe it was the smile he was wearing, maybe it was the intensity in his eyes.

Oh, God.

Cassandra was now smelling a fait accompli. "Who are you, some superhero? Where did you go? There was no tux in the car. And shoes? Look! Where are your boots?"

It was easier to make jokes than to face the panic

that she was feeling. There was something very magical about the way he looked, the way she felt. Magic had no place in her life.

"Ready to go?" he asked, presenting her with his arm and completely ignoring her reaction.

Which didn't make her happy.

The restaurant was right on the lake. A very nice continental place that she'd been to more times than she could count, but she didn't want to spoil his fun, so she kept quiet. Then she noticed the absence of people. Candles were glittering on the tables, but no one was around.

More panic. "Slow night, huh?" she said to the maître d'.

He merely smiled at her and led them out onto the patio. "Here you are, Mr. Barclay."

Cassandra swallowed hard as full-blooded fear zapped through her. There were candles everywhere, a light breeze hitting out from the lake and along the water's edge. The skyline of Chicago loomed overhead. A few boats were out on the water, their lights shining and reflecting like stars in the night sky.

She blinked rapidly. Dust was getting in her eye.

"Are you okay?" he asked. He, who looked absolutely gorgeous in black. He, who currently looked at her as if she wasn't U.S.D.A. prime, but like she was Empress of the World. He, who currently looked like a man in love.

Cassandra just wasn't that strong. Her heart tripped over itself, once, twice.

"Everything is beautiful. Thank you," she said, remembering her manners.

He held out her seat, just as the steward came forth with his offering of champagne. Pop. Fizz. Two glasses full.

She didn't know what to say.

Then the violin began. A single tone floating in the air. She had no idea of what song it was, but she was going to remember it forever.

"I hope you don't mind. I just didn't feel like dealing with a crowd tonight."

And so, whoosh, he makes the crowd disappear. "I forget you're a Barclay sometimes."

He smiled that generous smile she was starting to think of as familiar. "That's the nicest thing you've ever said."

"You don't want to be a Barclay?" she asked.

"It's not quite what everyone thinks. Dad wants us to make it on our own. He's from that new school of thought, 'kick your kids out and make them fly.'"

She looked around. "You fly well. What's the special occasion?" she asked.

"Just being with you." He lifted his glass.

Helplessly she drank and lost herself in the night darkness of his eyes. "Oh, my."

"I spent all day thinking about you, thinking about being with you."

"Noah, don't," she said, because she was terrified of what she would say in return.

"We don't have to talk. Dance with me."

He held her close, and the solitary music guided them around the patio, the soulful sound wrapping around them. It was so isolated, so far removed from everything else. When he stopped, cupped her face and kissed her, she couldn't help it. She started to cry.

Gently, he wiped away her tears. "You know I love you, don't you?" he asked.

She nodded, because she could see it there. There was desire, but there was something much more. "I'm not going to say anything back," she said, wiping at her eyes. The whole scene felt wrong, as if she'd been dropped into someone else's life, not her own.

He smiled and kissed her. It was one small kiss, as soft as the summer breeze that was blowing on her skin. "You take your time, sweetheart. I'm in no rush."

"I don't think I can do this."

He laughed softly. "That I don't believe, even for

one minute. You do whatever you put your mind to. I just want you to put your mind to this. To us."

He stopped and kissed her. It was one of his sneaky, touchy-feely kisses that just made her want to cry more.

The food was delicious, not that she could have told anyone what she ate. He told her stories about his travels, about his antique sword collection, about his father's cigars.

"You'll meet them soon," he said, another fait accompli.

Then it was time to go. He wrapped his arm around her as they stepped outside, waiting for the valet to bring his car around.

"You aren't like any of the others," she said.

"I told you that a long time ago. You just now starting to figure it out?"

She nodded and he kissed her again. "Don't worry. I can steamroll an elephant if necessary. A Barclay can do a lot when they get into it."

She smiled, his confidence contagious. "And you're 'into it' now?"

He grinned. "I'm just getting started."

THAT NIGHT he took her to his apartment. It wasn't a penthouse or a loft downtown, but it was a good place. He called it home. And now that she was here, it was home. He made coffee and when she stood in the kitchen, she reached to the back of her dress, starting to get undressed.

He grabbed her hands before they got too far. He was determined to have her trust him. Every time they got too heavy on the relationship, she went right back to sex.

"You're forgetting about my rules, aren't you?"

Using his most patient sigh, he led her back to the living room and sat her down on the couch. "Tell me about your day."

She blinked. "I thought this was the culminating moment. A little romance, a little lovemaking."

"We'll get there. You're rushing me again. Tell me about your day."

And she did, slowly at first, and then she warmed up, telling him about her visit from one of the diamond sellers, telling him how Spawn was eating up her shopping allowance in dog food, and then finally laughing as she told him about Kimberly's new love.

Some heavy weight lifted from his shoulders as he watched her face. She came alive. Her smile came easier. Eventually, he couldn't wait any longer.

A man could only have so much patience around her; Noah knew the beauty that lay underneath her dress.

However, he was slow and caring. When he carried her to his bed, he remembered all his fantasies that had stayed with him for so long. It was odd because he didn't expect to fall in love with her, but here she was, bare in his bed, her dark hair falling over her breasts, just as he'd dreamed. But he hadn't anticipated the rush of feeling that he felt. The protectiveness. He took his time with her. Mindful that this was a seduction, just as surely as the other times had been.

But she was changing, too. This time she didn't get mad at him. No, this time she was content to let him pleasure her. Her sighs were sweet music to him. He forced his body to wait as he played her, teased her, loved her.

When she opened her eyes, languorous and heavy, she watched him with a dreamy smile on her face. Noah swallowed. Hard.

Men would slay themselves, slay each other for just the hope of that single intimate smile. Noah had already seen it happen, he was already paying the price, but his heart was sure.

Then he slid inside her, moving slow and easy, and she gave a contented smile.

His eyes slid over her, possessively, knowing that tonight she was his.

"There you are. Let me love you, Cassandra."

And as he moved inside her, he knew that no man would ever touch her again.

CASSANDRA WOKE UP to the sound of his voice. The sky was still dark, the clock said it was 3:00 a.m., and he was talking on the phone.

She snuck quickly into the bathroom and checked the mirror, gasping at the horror that stared back at her. She fixed the smeared mascara, unhappy that she'd forgotten her makeup. As a rule, she was never seen sans makeup.

She looked carefully at the woman who looked back. There was a softness that wasn't normally there. She scrubbed at her face until the softness was gone. Then she heard him hang up the phone and she ran and climbed into bed before he came back. This time she pretended to be asleep.

"MISS WARD, somebody's here to see you," Kim yelled as she came into the work area, "and he's hot, too."

And that would be Noah. Cassandra smiled. He had said he might stop by. She pulled out her compact and dabbed a bit of shimmer powder on her face.

When she walked out to the front, she stopped. It wasn't Noah. Today's visitor was Benedict, complete with a single red rose.

She took a deep breath, willing herself to stay calm. "Hello."

"I came to see you. You wouldn't pick up my calls."

"Gotta love Caller ID," she said.

"You're making the papers again."

"Why are you here?"

"Because you have to talk to me. I have turned my life upside down to come back here, to try again. I've learned. Is it so hard for you to just talk?"

"I don't believe in second chances. You knew the rules. Strike one and you're out. Besides, I'm not sure if I really believe that you believe I was telling the truth about David."

He hesitated. The rat bastard hesitated.

She jumped all over it. "See, you still don't believe me and that was eight years ago. You divorce your wife—why she married you, I don't know—move back here, and to top it all off, you don't even believe me...now. How stupid is that, Benedict?"

He laid the rose down on the counter. "How am I supposed to forget about you?"

Cassandra closed her eyes. She had been dreading this day ever since he'd moved back to Chicago. "It's not even about me. This is all about the sex. Just find another warm, willing body. Trust me, Benedict, I'm right." As the words poured out of her, she realized it was true. Every relationship she'd had with a man had been based solely on sex. Except for one.

"Ah, Cassie, you've changed. When did you get so tough? Did Barclay do that to you?"

She crossed her arms. "No, Benedict. I've been

tough since I was fourteen, you just missed it. Look, you're wasting your time."

"Because of Noah?"

"Yes," she said, smiling. "Yes."

"He's going to be very, very angry when he loses his right to bid."

"Huh?"

"I'm the oversight director, Cassie. I find oversights. You know that construction project that he's so hot for? Oops. I bet I could find an oversight if I tried."

She shook her head. "No, Benedict. Go back to work, find somebody new."

He ran a hand through his hair. "I could do it, you know."

"You're not a blackmailer. You used to be a good man."

He pushed the rose toward her. "That's for you. I'm not going to give up."

Cassandra touched his hand. "Benedict. Don't ruin your life here. I'm really not worth it. You think it would work between us, but it wouldn't."

"It did at one time."

She smiled. "You were my first love, you'll always be my first love. For a long time I hated you for what you did, but it wouldn't have mattered."

"I'm not giving up."

Cassandra sighed. Had he always been such a

child? When she'd known him she'd been a child, as well, but she had managed to grow up. "I have to go back to work."

"I'll see you again," he said, and he walked out the door.

NOAH SPOTTED O'Malley coming from Cassandra's store. At first he stopped, sure that he'd made a mistake. Then he realized that yes, it was Benedict, and he shouldn't be surprised that Benedict was there.

Noah knew how the man felt about Cassandra. If a man wanted to see Cassandra, he went to the one place that she couldn't dodge him: her store. Noah knew that because he'd done it himself.

He took a deep breath because Noah was a logical, rational man, and he wasn't going to let this bother him.

He walked in, pleased to see her out front.

"Good afternoon. Ready for lunch?" he asked, which actually translated to, Why was your ex-fiancé here?

"Yeah. Give me just a minute. Kim, I'm heading out for lunch." Which wasn't the answer he was looking for.

"All right. Take as loooong as you need."

Cassandra looped around the counter and held out her hand automatically, but not before Noah noticed the rose.

"A secret admirer?" he joked.

"No," said Cassandra, and didn't say anything else.

They ate at a sidewalk café at the edge of the lake, which he had chosen on purpose to remind her of the other night. She smiled at him, even kissed him twice, but she didn't say one word about Benedict, and by the time she ordered dessert, it *was* starting to bother him. He could come right out and ask her, but then it would look like he didn't trust her, and he did.

Finally, he shoved Benedict O'Malley back to the furthest recesses of his mind and enjoyed their lunch. As he walked her to her store, he was a little more charming than normal, a little wittier. And when he left her, he kissed her with just a little more anger than love.

10

HER FATHER OWNED a cabin in Minnesota. It was only a five-hour drive from Chicago when a man's intent on his destination. Noah took his time.

He noticed that she didn't say much about her father or Benedict, instead talking about her new pair of shoes—not that he was really interested; baseball—he was a basketball man, didn't back losers; and the finer points in choosing dog food—apparently Spawn was putting on weight.

Noah didn't press her. He just let her talk and eventually they were driving through the backwoods to find her father's summer cabin.

Her father wasn't quite what Noah expected. For some reason he was anticipating a larger-than-life boisterous version of Cassandra. Instead, Jozef Ward was a small man with wire spectacles and a longish, graying beard.

"Come in, come in," he said, giving his daughter an affectionate hug. "Welcome. And who are you?" he asked, turning to Noah.

"Dad, this is Noah Barclay."

Her father nodded. "Oh." Then he waved his hands toward the Adirondack chairs. "Sit, sit, sit. You've been driving all this way, you must be pooped."

They all sat down, and Noah waited for Cassandra to say something.

"So," said Jozef. "How is business?"

"We did well for the month. I brought the statements to you."

He turned to Noah. "She's a good daughter. Not only looks, but brains, too. Got the brains from her mother. God rest her soul," he said, tapping his head.

"That's enough," said Cassandra, who was blushing, or at least Noah assumed the red flush on her cheeks was a blush, not that he'd ever seen her blush before.

"So, is this serious?"

Cassandra interrupted before Noah could answer. "I'm going to stop visiting you if you can't behave. Noah is a friend."

Noah shot her a look.

"A very good friend," she corrected.

"You think an old man can't see things, no?"

"You're not an old man, and you can still cut better than most of the shlemiels on 47th Street."

Jozef turned to Noah. "You see why I love her?"

"Dad!"

Her father buried his face in his hands. "All right, all right. Deny an old man his fun, why don't you? How is Liepshutz? Old man Thompson called and said he saw some stones at forty percent below Rapaport prices."

Her face fell. "I haven't seen him."

"What? He was going on a buying trip. I told him to bring you the best of the best." He turned to Noah. "He loves my girl. I'll call him and find out what's what."

"No," said Cassandra.

"Why not?"

"Wait until September when you come back, then call."

The old man peered behind his spectacles. "You're not getting along with Liepshutz?"

"No."

"But he kept asking me, 'When are you leaving for the summer, Jozef? When are you leaving for the summer?' I don't understand this."

Cassandra folded her hands in her lap and smiled tightly. "Can we leave this alone now?"

"Well, I suppose we could, but I still don't understand it."

"I can handle it," Cassandra assured him. "Sanderson had some nice canary diamonds that I can work with, and Aznar had a natural fancy vivid yellow and I picked up an intense blue, as well."

"It's such a girly thing, wanting those fancies. I remember the day when brilliant solitaires in platinum was all that mattered."

"The business is changing?" asked Noah, steering the conversation safely away from Liepshutz. It was just that one more thing that he didn't know about her.

Jozef waved a hand. "Like a kaleidoscope. Women, they want colors now! My girl, she spotted that one early."

They stayed over lunch, Cassandra making sandwiches, and in general, playing hostess, which was an odd thing, but the dynamics between father and daughter were odd, as well.

"What do you do, Mr. Barclay?" her father asked in between bites of his lunch.

"I'm in construction."

Jozef raised one grizzled gray brow, got that hoity-toity look in his eyes, and now Noah knew where she got it from.

"He owns his own company, Dad."

Jozef waved a hand. "I knew that. What do you build?"

"Bridges, roads."

"He's bidding on a project for the city."

"Are they finally fixing the Hillside Strangler? And they call it a freeway? The only thing free is the heartburn.

"You're staying for dinner?"

Cassandra shook her head. "We have to get back."

Jozef nodded. "I remember when I was young and in love with your mother. We usually had to get back, too. I'll be back at the end of August, early September at the latest. You take care of things, and don't let Sanderson take you for a dime more than needs to be paid. Oh, she's a good one. Since she started at the store, business has doubled. Doubled!"

Noah looked at Cassandra, surprised. She wasn't usually shy about claiming credit for her own accomplishments. "Really?"

"The day she was born, I was crushed. I wanted a boy so badly. I'm a man, what do I know about girls? But Helen knew. I thought, a girl who polishes diamonds? Never'll happen. And look. It happened."

"You must be very proud of her."

Her father glowed as he reached for Cassandra and planted a kiss on either cheek. "I am."

SHE SHOULDN'T have taken him to visit Dad. She never introduced her father to anyone because her father never failed to embarrass her and in some ways drill little pinholes through her that enabled people to see right in. *That* bothered her. "I hope you didn't mind my dad."

Noah shook his head. "You haven't met my family. I understand. He's very proud of you, though."

Yeah, he was proud of her. She was a means to an end. She was the winning lottery ticket he never bought. It usually didn't bother her. Today it bothered her.

"What happened to your mother?"

"Heart attack when I was little."

"I'm sorry."

"It's okay."

His hand reached out and took hers in a strong, comforting grip. She liked that about him, that he knew just the right way to touch her. Most men didn't.

He didn't ask things of her, he only gave. It was so easy to be around him. She could truly be herself and let down her guard.

Because she loved him.

It was time that she admitted that bit of truth to herself.

She looked over at him, at the hands that had cherished her, at the mouth that had adored her, never asking anything in return.

"Can you pull off for a minute?" she asked.

He looked at her right away. "Are you okay?"

She nodded. "Yes, I'm wonderful. Over there," she said, pointing to a dirt road that ran alongside the main one.

He pulled to a stop. "What is it?"

"I want you to make love to me."

And Noah, because he was Noah, immediately caught the difference. One more reason to love him. "You coming 'round to my way of thinking?" he asked, with a cheeky grin.

"I think so, but you have to convince me."

He gave a whoop and pulled her close, kissing her in that way that he did—long, lingering, as if he couldn't live without her.

"Don't ever, *ever* get bucket seats, hmm."

ON FRIDAY, Noah invited her to dinner with his family, and, with only minutes to spare, she was ready. She spent two hours on her makeup and hair—a European facial and an emergency appointment with her hair stylist, Francois.

When Noah showed up at her door, he put his hand to his heart. "Oh, Cassandra. I hope that's easy to put back together," and then he grabbed her to him and planted one right on her. He damaged the lipstick, smudged the foundation and dislodged the powder.

She forgave him.

His father was a big bear of a man, who at first scared her, until she saw him cower when Suzanne Barclay yelled at him for his cigars. It was a nice moment. His sister Joan was there, with her fiancé, Harry.

"Miss Ward," said Joan with a beady velociraptor look in her eyes.

"Joan, behave," said Noah, a threat in his voice.

"You wouldn't do anything. Besides, Harry would defend me in a flash."

Harry shook his head. "No. I have to live with you. I couldn't get away with it myself, but *he* could."

She glowered at him, but then he grabbed her hand and something passed between them. Cassandra recognized that look.

Noah leaned in close. "Don't let her scare you. She's all claws."

Cassandra tilted back her head, her throat exposed, indicating complete confidence. Then she leaned over to whisper in his ear, "Honey, there's not a woman alive I can't take down in claw-to-claw combat."

Suzanne moved them all to the sitting room for pre-dinner drinks, and Cassandra went over to Joan, mainly to show off her newly acquired magnanimous disposition. Love could do that to a woman.

"Who did your ring?" asked Cassandra, professional curiosity getting the better of her.

"Saulis," she said, holding out her hand for Cassandra's inspection.

Cassandra took a long look. She would have put Joan in an emerald cut with a hint of red to show off her complexion, but this one was good. "It's nice. You've got the great hands to carry it off."

Joan relaxed. "Really? Not that I'm surprised or anything."

Cassandra smiled. "Of course."

"So who does your hair? It's fabulous. I keep mine long, but I have trouble getting the ends right."

"Francois on West Maple. He can do miracles."

Joan considered it. "Maybe some highlights?"

Cassandra nodded. "No one will ever know."

And so they bonded.

"It's scary," said Noah to Harry. "Two alpha she-cats in a moment of togetherness. All it took was hair secrets."

"Joan's been dying to meet her since they put that picture of the dress in the paper. I told her she should buy one." Harry frowned. "She didn't see the brilliance in that idea."

Noah laughed.

"How's the transportation project coming?"

"I turned in all my papers yesterday. There's a big meeting next week."

Cassandra perked up then. "So everything's going okay?"

Noah nodded confidently, as usual, and she gave a sigh of relief. She hadn't thought Benedict would make trouble, but still, she had worried.

NOAH'S FATHER took him aside, surreptitiously to talk just among the men, but Noah knew it was because he wanted to sneak a cigar. They moved to the solarium, where his father settled himself in his favorite chair, clipped his cigar and lit up his favorite vice.

"Is she going to give you any trouble?"

"Cassandra? Probably."

His father tapped the ashes into the plant. "That's a good sign. A man doesn't truly appreciate his own sex until dealing with a self-assured woman. You're going to have your hands full with that one."

And didn't Noah know it. She was a challenge, a headache and the rest of his life all rolled into one. "You taught me never to just settle, Dad."

His father laughed. "That's the truth. You've done good. Makes a man proud of his own. I was worried when you took off right out of college. In my day, the kids went to Woodstock, not halfway around the world."

But that's what Noah loved. Travel books were for the faint of heart. A man who stayed in one place too long was prone to tunnel-vision. Judging everything on appearances. Noah had learned to look a little deeper. "I had to start somewhere."

"Now that you're home, you might have the most difficult problems of all. I saw the look in your eyes when you were talking about the bid. I can step in, help you out."

Noah shook it off. "No. I've got everything under control."

"All right, but you tell me if you need something. I've got friends, son."

"I know you do, but so do I."

"Yeah, but you keep an eye on them when Cassandra's around. She'll make a man forget his own loyalties."

Hell, she could make a man forget his own name when she put her mind to it, but that's one of the reasons he had fallen for her in the first place. "She can handle herself."

His father pressed the cigar into the potted plant. There'd be hell to pay when Noah's mother found it in the morning, but they'd work through it. They always did. "I haven't seen you this serious before."

"I hadn't met her before."

"That's the way of it?"

"That it is."

"I SAW BENEDICT at your store last week." Noah blurted after they'd gotten back to her place, because he thought this was something they needed to discuss. Okay, mainly it was something he needed to discuss because it was driving him nuts.

Her expression said the topic was closed, the don't-ask-don't-tell look that he couldn't bear. "So?"

"Why didn't you tell me?"

Frowning, she collapsed on her couch. "Because it wasn't important. He's nothing. It's nothing. If you trusted me, you'd know that."

"I love you." He stood silent, waiting for her to reciprocate. Nothing. Noah shook off the feeling of disquiet. That was okay, he was a patient man. He could wait.

"I want to know if he's bothering you," he said, primarily to fill the silence.

"So you can go take care of him for me? Going to go beat him up, Noah?"

"If that's what it takes," he answered. He wanted her to need him, wanted her to trust him with her problems, and she didn't.

"I can handle him. I've been handling it all my life," she said, trying to act tough. The confidence that he normally loved in her was now his own worst enemy.

"Cassandra, I'm here for you. You don't have to handle it all by yourself."

"Because you don't trust me?"

"Damn it, no. Because I want to help you." He ground his fingers into his palms, wishing he knew the magic words, wishing he knew the perfect way to break through the diamond-hard barriers that she was using to keep him at arm's length.

"I don't need help. Leave it alone."

"Will you tell me if he comes to see you again?"

"No."

"And what happens if he threatens you? Or something worse? Then would you tell me?"

Silence.

"Why?" he asked.

"Because it wouldn't solve anything and eventually I'd be the one who's blamed."

"If you loved me—"

"Don't do it, Noah."

"What?"

"You're slipping into 'every man.' I thought you wanted to be different. You said you didn't want to rush things, that you were content to wait it out. Changed your mind?"

He sat down next to her. Frustration and understanding sparred inside him. He closed his eyes until slowly the feelings ebbed away. "I haven't changed my mind, but it takes two people to make a relationship, Cassandra. I can't carry it all by myself forever."

"If you're unhappy, you can leave."

He took her in his arms, held her and loved her. In the end, that was all he could do. Hopefully it would be enough. "Just try, Cassandra. Promise me that you'll try."

She lifted her head and met his lips, which soothed the ache inside him. It was a long time later before he realized that she'd never answered him at all.

THE NEXT MORNING Noah went to see Benedict. It wasn't something that he had planned. It wasn't something he even wanted to do, but he found himself doing it, anyway.

"I came by to make sure the tax forms were to spec."

Benedict leaned back in his chair, his whole manner reeking of arrogance. "I don't know."

Noah nearly decked him right there. "Can you call down to purchasing or accounting or whoever would know and find out?"

"Something wrong, Barclay? You seem tense today."

"I have followed every procedure that you laid out, I have met every deadline that you have set, and haven't said a word. I'm not going to stand around with my thumb up my ass anymore."

"You got it bad, don't you?"

"Stay away from her," Noah said.

"For me, it was like drinking lighter fluid—bitter to swallow—and it just takes one little match, then your insides are on fire. It burns you up and no one knows. You can't fool me. I've been there."

Noah hated him. Right then and there, he could

have killed him. His hands fisted and he was ready to hit him. Hit him, until the bastard's blood was warming his hands. Noah closed his eyes, got his emotions under control and flung open the office door.

"See you around, Barclay."

"Stay away from her."

Benedict just laughed.

EMIL PRITZKER came around once a month. He had connections at either De Beers or the Mafia, but he always had good, legal stones at rock-bottom prices.

He showed up at Ward & Ward on Wednesday, just as Kimberly was going out to lunch with Mark.

"Hey, girlie! How youse doing today?"

Cassandra liked Emil because a) he was from New York, like her, and sometimes she missed it and b) he talked with a high, whiny voice that made her feel like she was flirting with Bugs Bunny. Bugs Bunny she could handle any day of the week.

"Pull up a stool," said Cassandra.

"Business is good?" he asked, fishing his glasses out from his pocket.

"You're here to talk business? I thought you were coming to make time with me."

Emil laughed. "Oh, no, girlie. You'd cleave through my heart just like it was a 2-carat emerald cut." He pulled out the bags of diamonds and placed them on the tray.

Cassandra pulled out her loupe and examined each one. "You'll be in love with someone else next week."

"So my wife keeps hoping. How's your father?"

Cassandra picked up the canary diamond and examined it. Nice. Very, very nice. "I'm going to see him next week. Got a message?"

"Tell him I want that fifty bucks he owes me."

"When's the last time you played poker with my dad?"

"Ninety-six," said Emil, but he pointed to his head. "I've got a good memory. Gingko."

"I'll tell him."

Cassandra pointed to the diamond. "Tell me about this one. I like it. How much do you want?"

Let the games begin.

"Five grand."

Cassandra coughed. "Excuse me while I die here. Five grand? It can't be more than a G in color and that crack inside there makes the Grand Canyon look small. Fifteen hundred tops."

Emil tsk-tsked, his bottom lip curling up to completely obliterate the top one. "You can use those looks on some other man, Miss Cassandra, but they won't work with me. Four grand, but that's my final offer."

Cassandra closed her arms across her chest. Classic nonreceptive. "You're going to need a crazy pill as well as gingko for those prices. Nobody on this row will give you that."

"Thirty-five hundred," he said, then shook a finger at her. "But that's my final offer."

"Twenty-seven fifty. We'll split the difference."

He laid a hand over his heart. "She got me again. Twenty-seven fifty, but you're taking my shirt."

After Emil left, Cassandra cataloged the new diamonds into inventory and settled down to work.

Pbbbbtttt. The door buzzer sounded. Maybe Kimberly was back from lunch, or maybe it was a customer.

Neither. It was Sidney Liepshutz. Out of all her customers and vendors, Sidney was the one most likely to be discovered a homicidal psychopath.

"Ah, Cassandra. I told your father I would come by to see you while he was gone."

"Too late, Sidney. Emil was just here. Bought all the stock we needed."

"He can't beat my prices, you know that. And for you, an extra twenty-five percent, just because you're my favorite."

Cassandra toyed with the idea of actually looking at his stones, simply because it was a great deal. Then she looked up into the pale blue of his eyes and didn't like what she saw there.

"Sorry, I'm not interested. Come back, later, maybe in a couple of years. Two, twenty, fifty?"

"Why do you not like me, Cassandra?"

"Men like you gave me nightmares in high school,

Liepshutz. I don't have them anymore, but I avoid creepy men when I get the chance."

He reached out to touch her and she drew back before his icky flesh could actually contaminate her own. "You can leave now."

"Sure, sure. Not a problem."

She walked around the counter and marched to the front, opening the door.

"You should be nicer," he said.

"Not in this lifetime."

She swallowed the bile in her mouth and stared into the icy paleness of his eyes, determined to send him on his way.

"Your father will hear about this."

"You bet he will. Cause I'm going to tell him. Don't mess with me, Liepshutz."

Just then Kimberly walked through the door, eyeing the defeated Liepshutz with wariness. "You need me to get something, Cassandra?"

"Nah. He was just leaving."

And he did just that. Cassandra heaved a huge sigh.

"That was so cool! I saw it from the window. Where did you learn to stare a guy down like that?"

"It's Survival 101. But I've been doing it for a long time, so it just comes more naturally to me."

"Could you show me?"

"Sure, but I need to finish the Forsythe setting."

"Oh, yeah, and Mr. Barclay called earlier. He'll be here at three. Said he had a meeting downtown and he thought he'd come by to say hi." Kimberly smiled. "I think he's wanting more than just to say hi."

Cassandra couldn't wait. Right now, she needed somebody clean to hold her and kiss her, and make her forget all about Liepshutz the Creepshutz.

She needed Noah.

NOAH FINISHED his meeting with the bank. All the appropriate credit lines were now in place. He had picked up a couple of small jobs for Anvil. They were nothing to write home about, but provided good solid work. The transportation bid was big opportunity, but he knew it wasn't wise to put all his eggs in one basket. He had every "i" dotted, and every "t" crossed, so there wasn't much left to do but wait for the selection of bidders to be announced.

It seemed he'd been doing a lot of waiting recently, which immediately put him in mind of Cassandra. So he stopped by the store to see if he could tempt her into a cup of coffee. As they walked out of her shop, she tucked her hand in his. That was a first.

"You okay?" he asked, not that he was going to complain or anything.

"I'm marvelous now," she said with a contented smile.

"How's your day?"

"Good. I bought four diamonds from my favorite dealer and finished the setting for the Forsythe ring. And now you're here. What could be more perfect?"

"I don't think anything could."

"How's Anvil? Ready to take the city by storm?"

"I picked up a little contract this morning. We were just finalizing the financing at the bank."

"Congratulations. We should celebrate."

"We could do something special tonight."

"Why don't you just come by my house? We can order pizza."

She was using the red-hot tone, that one that always gave him an instant hard-on. Noah stopped, pulled her against the nearest wall. "You do this on purpose, don't you? Just to see me squirm."

"Sometimes," she said, shooting him a coy, sideways glance. Then her face changed, got urgent and afraid. "Kiss me, Noah."

And he did. They got some car honks, a few snickers and assorted ribald comments, but he kissed her. Right in the middle of the city, simply because she needed him. It was the first time that he felt like he was something more than just a willing man to her.

Waiting for her was starting to pay off. He was slowly beginning to think that she'd shed the misguided impression she had of herself.

When he lifted his head, he smoothed back her hair. "Better?"

"Much. We need to get back before Kimberly gives the store away."

"Sure thing."

EVERYTHING WAS FINE until Kimberly felt the need to provide commentary on Cassandra's earlier visit from Creepshutz.

"You should have seen her. It was like watching Laura Croft, you know. Before he knew what was happening the man was down."

Noah stared at Cassandra and she winced at the hurt in his eyes. "Oh, yeah. She can really take care of herself, can't she? I wish I'd been here."

"It wouldn't have mattered. Not with the way she dealt with him."

"No, I guess not."

"Kimberly, why don't you go into the back room," said Cassandra, knowing that this was about to turn into an argument and she didn't want to do it in front of the children.

"Sure thing, boss," said Kimberly, punching into the air several times.

"She's being dramatic."

"You didn't say a word."

"You'd get mad."

"I wouldn't get mad."

"You're mad now."

"Only because you never tell me these things. How much goes on that I don't know about, Cassandra? How much of your life am I completely missing?"

"Just the bad stuff."

"Is it so impossible to let me inside?"

Cassandra shrugged. "You're inside a lot."

"That doesn't mean much to you."

It would have been easier if he had just yelled at her. And it would have hurt a helluva lot less. "Why don't you leave?"

He caught her close. "Cassandra, I'm sorry. I said that badly and I'm not leaving with this between us. You keep all your problems locked away. You're not shy with your body, but you're shy about everything else. When most people care about other people, they let them inside."

She hated the tone, the look of disappointment in his eyes. "I'm not most people."

"You got that right. But so what? I want to be there for you, always, maybe not physically, okay, maybe physically, but I want us to have something more than sex."

"I'll try," Cassandra promised.

MONDAY was her day off. Usually, Cassandra had a two-hour moisturizer, a bikini wax, and sweated off three pounds while lying nude in the afternoon sun. She stopped sunbathing in the nude after she got Spawn. What used to be hedonistic was now "icky." Instead, they would head to the park.

Cassandra kept hoping that someone would claim the big, black beast, but no one had so far. Secretly, she suspected she was stuck with him. Even more secretly, she was glad.

She took him to Bark Park on the lakefront. It was a special treat, and one that she kept to herself. It would ruin her ball-buster image if it got out that she was just another indulgent dog owner.

Technically, there were leash-laws. Untechnically, no one obeyed them here. Just as she was throwing the Frisbee to him, her cell rang.

"Where were you on Monday night? I tried to call you, but you weren't there. At midnight, at one, and at four a.m."

"I do not believe you called at 4:00 a.m., Beth," said Cassandra, too smart to fall for that one.

"Well, if I had called at four, would you have been there?"

"Of course," lied Cassandra. Beth, Mickey and Jess all knew that she never spent the night. Another rule. But it was one mainly because she had yet to let a man see her without her makeup. Except Noah. It was all about the image.

"Spencer's got a dinner on Friday night. It's some

journalistic awards hoo-haw. I need a dress. Do you have something that I could borrow? I'm thinking something that's not so Little Bo Peep."

"The flames are already dying?"

"Bite your tongue. We have flames that are—flaming. I just like to give him a heart attack when he becomes too complacent. You know, 'Behind Closed Doors—How My Domesticated Cat Turned Sex Kitten.'"

Cassandra rolled her eyes. Beth practiced her own special kind of journalism: confession writing. "Meet me in two hours. We'll find something for you," she instructed. Then she remembered the peacock-blue D&G that she'd bought last year. "I know just the thing. But I need something in return."

"Name it."

"Spencer's been covering the transportation contract, right? Ask him if Benedict can cause trouble with Noah's bid."

"You don't think...?"

"Yeah, I think," she answered.

"Nancy Drew, reporting for service."

"Don't let on to Spencer who's asking. I don't want Noah to suspect I'm worried."

"Sure thing."

THEY ENDED UP trying on clothes, sharing a pitcher of martinis between them. A deadly combination.

The blue dress was perfect on Beth, just like Cassandra knew it would be, and she gave Beth lessons on flirting.

"So this is how you do it?" asked Beth while she coyly sucked on a finger and stared at her reflection in the mirror.

"You tell my secrets, and you'll die an ugly, painful death."

"Tell me about Noah. Are you in luh-uv?" said Beth, being very annoying.

"No," answered Cassandra. Before yesterday, she might have said yes. She would have been going into exquisite detail over every small thing that he'd told her, waxing lyrically about how perfect he was. Now she had to keep all that to herself because paradise just didn't exist for her.

"Have you been on dates? With non-Noah men types?"

"Of course I have," said Cassandra.

The phone rang. It was Mickey.

"Martin? Darling!"

"I told you. This is Mickey. I will not be used—"

"I had a great time Thursday night." She laughed in her sexy, baby-doll voice.

"Is Noah there? Are you trying to make him jealous. I swear I'm going to call the man myself and tell him—"

"It was only one time," purred Cassandra, "and you're such a good friend."

"Do you turn Jessica into Josiah? Uh, no I don't think so. Or Beth? Is Beth a Bob? No. It's just me."

And then Beth hit the speaker phone button and Mickey's tirade blasted into the room.

"S'all right, Mickey. The game's up. She's been caught. Red-handed. Well, missy?" asked Beth tapping her foot. "Why the ruse?"

Cassandra shifted on her feet. It was a classic sign of discomfort. "I was just having fun."

"Oh, that's rich," yelled Mickey. "Cruelty at my expense."

"I was with Noah Thursday night."

"Tell us something we didn't know," said Beth. "Harry told Spencer at work this morning, who immediately called me and told me because he loves me."

"You knew! Why didn't you say something?"

"I wanted to see if you'd confess all or whether you were going to pull a Cassandra and lie."

"Oh, that is *so* unfair," grumbled Cassandra. She was supposed to be enigmatic, mysterious, imageful. Instead she was an open book. God.

"Have y'all been drinking?" asked Mickey. "And was I invited? No."

"She's helping me pick out a dress for Spencer."

Mickey started to laugh, that oh-yeah laugh of experience.

"You can come over if you want. We've still got a quarter of a pitcher left. Oh, I forgot. You're not drinking. Preggers yet?"

"I told you. We're not trying to get pregnant. I just don't drink anymore."

"All right, we'll let you off the hook. I owe you, Mick."

"It's Michelle to you, sister," said Mickey, and then she hung up.

"She's so sensitive," said Cassandra.

"Oh, yeah, right. Like you're not. Lying to cover it up. Don't think you're off the hook. I'm on to you now. That's fidelity. That's monogamy. Because of him."

"Him who?"

"Want me to spell it out? N-O-H-A."

"N-O-A-H," corrected Cassandra.

"Oh, yeah, just pick on me because I'm blond. What's his deal?"

"There is no deal."

"This is serious."

"It's not serious."

"It's ma-nah-ga-mous," carefully enunciating each syllable, each one a sword into Cassandra's side. "Do we need to reread Cassandra's rules for sex?"

"All right, enough. You're right. I've been faithful. Can we move on?"

Beth crossed her arms over her chest and leaned back in a traditional victor pose. "Well, well, well. I didn't think I'd see the day."

"Are you going to help me find out about Benedict or not?"

Beth grinned. "Of course." Then she hugged Cassandra tight. "Oh, this is great. Cassandra's in love."

"Am not," lied Cassandra automatically.

But no one believed her.

11

ON TUESDAY, things started out bad and went downhill from there. The power had gone off twice in the morning, and Cassandra was alone in the shop. As soon as the Amesworth stone was done, she was going to close up herself.

Bbbzzzzzzztttttttttttttttt. And there it went again. Almost immediately the power came back on. Armed with nothing more than a really bad attitude, Cassandra stalked outside, prepared to sweet talk Mark into leaving the power alone.

Unfortunately, Mark wasn't there.

"What the hell are you doing?" she bellowed.

"Ah, jeez, lady, we're just doing our job," muttered the foreman, wearing his orange coveralls and orange hard hat.

"You've been at this for two weeks. Up and then down. My store goes into lockdown when the power goes off. Aspirin isn't going to cut it anymore. I'm developing a serious case of power rage here."

"Look, this is our last week. We're almost done. It was a nasty sewage pipe that needed fixing, and I have to be frank here, a sewage leak is going to be higher on the annoyance meter than these little power blips any day of the week."

"Then you'll leave?"

He nodded.

"And my power will be fine."

He nodded again.

"Okay, boys, go to it," she said, dusting her hands of the whole mess. Now, if it wasn't for the noise...although maybe a good pair of earplugs could fix that.

Cassandra spent the next hour setting the Amesworth stone. It was going to be a beautiful ring. Lola Amesworth would be very happy and no doubt her friends would be all agog over the piece and demand to know where she got it, and then Ward & Ward would be swamped with all the business...

Okay, sometimes she got ahead of herself. Cassandra pulled the stone from the dop and smiled. Just as she pulled out the box for it, she heard the buzzer. Customer. Hopefully a rich pop star who needed the world's biggest rock for...

Benedict.

Nothing like an ex-boyfriend to put a damper on daydreaming.

"I've got nothing else to say. Please leave."

"I'm not leaving this time."

"I'll call the cops."

"The list of bidders is announced tomorrow. I'm trying to decide about Noah's. You should be nicer to me."

"What do you want?"

"How are you doing? I don't think I got a chance to ask that yet."

"I'm fine. Gee, that's very nice and polite of you, but if it's all you wanted—"

He held up a hand. "I'm not done yet."

"If it involves body parts, the answer is no."

"Oh, Cass, you're wounding me here. Surely there was more to our relationship than sex. I mean, you did agree to marry me."

"No, Benedict, our relationship was all about sex. Why are you doing this? Is this some weird life crisis? Did you have a good life in...wherever you were?" she asked, even though she knew he'd been in Philly.

"I felt like I got off that path, Cass. Like I took a turn I wasn't supposed to. Samantha was a great woman, don't get me wrong, but I never felt like I was supposed to be married to her. I felt like I forced it, and the only thing I could trace it back to was you. I've never regretted a decision more—"

bbzzzzzztttttttttttttttt.

"What the hell is that?"

"The power. Just wait a minute. It'll be back on."

She held her breath. One minute turned into two.

Goddamn. Why now? Fifteen minutes passed but the power still wasn't on.

Benedict walked over to the door. "I'll go outside and get this straight—" he pulled at the door and it wouldn't budge.

"It's locked."

"You have keys."

"It's electronic."

"We're stuck," said Benedict. Always the bright one.

"There are rules here. I have a gun in the drawer and I won't hesitate to use it."

"Ah, Cassandra, I wouldn't hurt you and I'm not going to touch you—unless you want me to. But you gotta admit, this is like fate? You know, you being forced to listen to me."

"Are you trying to endear yourself to me, or trying to drive me to murder?"

"Fine. I'll leave you alone. Go back to work."

"Uh, there's no light."

Fifteen minutes turned into thirty. She called the power and the woman in customer service was really nice but also very clueless.

And then Noah called. Cassandra moved into the back room.

"Dinner tonight?" he asked.

"Sorry. Power's out here. I'm stuck for a bit."

"I could come down and wait with you."

"Don't be silly," she said. She would rather eat maggots than have Noah see Benedict. They'd fight, Noah would lose the bid, and the whole thing would reek.

Noah, being the stubborn man that he was, pressed forward. "I don't think it's silly, I think it's being supportive. Anything you need?"

"A hot bath when this is over."

"Candles, bubbles and champagne."

"I love you, Noah," she whispered. She might not have been completely honest about everything else, but this was the truth and not something to be said lightly.

"You mean that? I'll come down."

"No! I mean, you couldn't get in or anything. And just standing outside? That's crazy."

"Are you okay? Is something wrong?"

Cassandra gulped. "Everything's fine."

"Okay. Love you, too. Call me when you're free."

After she hung up, she went to the front, hoping that by some miracle either a) the power had come on or b) Benedict had magically disappeared. No such luck.

"That was Noah?" the nondisappearing Benedict asked.

She nodded.

"You love him, don't you?"

Another nod.

"He's not for you."

"He is."

"You think he trusts you?"

"He does."

"Did you tell him I was here?"

She kept her mouth shut.

"Not willing to risk it, are you?"

"Shut up, Benedict. Just shut up."

NOAH LEFT his office fifteen minutes early. Everything was lined up for the project. The list of bidders would be posted in the morning, and he'd done all he could. Now, it was just up to the fine city of Chicago.

He stopped by Marshall Field's on his way to her store. Perla lipstick in Soft Mauve. He knew it was her favorite lipstick, her favorite shade, and the best part was that he'd get to kiss it right off her. A win-win all 'round. Sometimes a man needed to get creative to please the woman he loved.

Her words on the phone had warmed him, made him hope.

He picked up a couple of sandwiches and dialed her cell just when he was outside her store.

"Cassandra? Power still out?"

"Do I sound happy?"

"No."

"There's your answer."

"I have something that will cheer you up."

"A brick flying through the window to break me out of this joint?"

"Just look outside—"

Noah stopped. A shadowy figure moved inside. Damn.

He watched as she stepped from the back room with cell phone in hand.

Benedict looked up, out the window. And waved.

Noah hung up his phone and walked off.

"HIS FAITH IN YOU is really amazing."

"Shut up."

Cassandra sat off by herself, huddled next to the hard glass of the counter. She should have said something. She should have told him the truth, but she'd never been one to admit weakness. She couldn't. Either the vultures would swoop in to take advantage or she would be blamed because she was too...too. Too sexy, too fun, too stacked. And so the circle went 'round and 'round.

Noah had made her think the circle was possibly coming to an end. For once she'd met a man who was strong enough to deal with it. So, she let him get closer than the requisite three feet. Once again, she'd screwed up.

Exactly one hour and seven minutes later the

power came back on. The lights blinked and then the buzzer crescendoed back to life.

"Get out," she muttered.

"No problem. I'm sorry things didn't work out for you, Cassandra. I told you he wasn't the right guy for you. You watch, he'll take off overseas again and you'll never hear from him."

"Go home, Benedict."

"Hey, I'll be there when you need somebody to pick up the pieces. I understand you better than anyone else."

"No, Benedict, you don't. You never did."

When she got home, there was one message on her answering machine. She stared at the blinking red light, already hearing his apology in her mind. A smile twitched at the corner of her mouth. That was the thing about Noah—he never had let her down. That was why she loved him. She punched the button.

"Cassandra, this is Jessica. Just wanted to know if I should bring the tequila tomorrow? I was thinking margaritas would be the perfect complement to a night of beauty and girl fun, don't you think? Call me and let me know."

Cassandra sank into a chair and let the numbness dilute the hurt. She needed that void, that emptiness, because she couldn't bear the stinging inside her.

Where was the steely bitch that she knew, loved and depended on in times of crisis?

Okay, so Noah had let her down, and what was she left with? The same thing she always had. Her friends.

She thought about canceling. She thought about spending the night alone, getting roaring drunk, or better yet, calling up one of the men listed in her black book as RWA: ready, willing and available. Revenge sex just wasn't in her makeup anymore. God, she had become such a sap.

ACCORDING TO THE CLOCK on her late-night cable television guide, when Noah called, it was 2:07 a.m.

"Why didn't you tell me he was there?" he started out, skipping right over hello.

"Because you would think it was my fault. He just showed up. Why did you leave? You just walked off."

"I would've killed him if I had stayed."

"Now do you understand why I kept my mouth shut?"

"What are we going to do?"

"I think we're already done," said Cassandra. "This is why I created my rules, Noah."

"You should have trusted me with the truth, but you don't. Every time a man comes around, you don't say a word to me. You just pull the shades down, so I don't know what's going on at all."

"You *think* there's something going on?"

"No, I want to trust you. I do trust you. But it's getting to me, I'm not going to lie about it. I stare at the drawn shades and can't help but wonder what I'm missing."

All along she had been strong, ready to bounce back after every knockdown, but this time she wasn't strong enough. God, she just wanted to be loved. Unfortunately, it wasn't in the cards.

She hung up on him.

THE NEXT MORNING, Noah went to city hall to find out whether or not the Chicago Department of Transportation considered Anvil worthy to bid on the transportation project. It was really all he had left.

He found the posting right away and scanned the names. And, no, Anvil wasn't one of them. Not that it really mattered to him. Right now, it was tough to give a shit about anything. And was this really a surprise?

No.

Why had he gone after her? She was a woman who went it alone. Always. That dream. Those dumb dreams.

He stuffed his hands into his pockets and went off

to find the nearest double-shot of whiskey. He looked at his watch. 9:07 a.m. A little early, but he cheered himself up with the thought that it was 11:07 p.m. somewhere in the world. That made it all right.

SPENCER CALLED NOAH that afternoon. "What are you doing tonight? My wife has ordered me to expand my social horizons."

"I wouldn't be very good company."

"That's all right. I never am."

"I'll meet you at eight."

JESSICA SHOWED UP first in sweats and with a fully stocked bar in a giant-size bag.

"Convenient," murmured Cassandra.

"You can never be too prepared."

"Or too drunk."

"Are you okay? You're missing something."

"Perhaps a buzz," said Cassandra, pulling out the bottle of tequila.

Jessica watched with wide eyes as Cassandra twisted off the lid and took a long swallow.

"Whoa! At this rate, I'm not letting you near my makeup."

"All it takes is a steady hand."

Then the doorbell rang. Mickey.

She was dressed in a miniskirt and heels. Cassandra took a step back.

"What's with the duds, Mick?"

"It's Michelle, thank you. And I was just tired of people forgetting."

"It's a good look for you," said Cassandra, nodding her head.

"A woman can never be too womanly," advised Mickey.

Jessica pulled out the glasses. "You're pregnant, aren't you? That's what all this is about."

"Can you stop with the pregnancy obsession? I'm not pregnant, I'm not trying to get pregnant."

Beth arrived just in time to prevent Baby Wars Round three, and in no time at all, Cassandra was settling into her old routine.

First, there was eye shadow correction for Jessica. "The color is all wrong. You need a gold, or a brown to bring out your skintone."

Next, a full skin-care regime for Beth. "You've been under stress, haven't you? There's an SOS written in your T-zone."

It felt comfortable, it felt good, it felt just like a shot of sedative right into the heart.

Just as she was feeling okay—that's what three shots of tequila can do for you—Beth pulled her aside.

"Noah's not on the bid list."

"What?"

"They 86ed Anvil."

"They can't do that," said Cassandra, forgetting for a split second that she was angry with him.

"Benedict did. He met with the city council in a closed session right before the list went up."

"I'm cursed, aren't I?"

"Uh, yeah. I'd really like to have some of your curse there, Cassandra."

"Never mind." Cassandra shut up and took another mind-busting shot of tequila. Playtime was over. Tomorrow she'd go see Benedict. She had screwed up Noah's bid, but maybe she could still make things right.

SPENCER SHOWED UP right on time, ordered a Scotch, and took out his pen. "We're running an article tomorrow about the possibility of impropriety in the bidding process."

"Can we not talk about that tonight?"

Spencer frowned. "Okay. I just thought that would be on your mind, and I could get some great quotes."

"I could give you great quotes, but none would be suitable for a family newspaper. It's over with anyway. Anvil will do fine. We just start out one small contract at a time."

"You don't sound upset."

"I've got other things on my mind."

"Is this where I should ask you about personal problems?"

"Why aren't women easier to deal with? I thought I could handle everything."

"If you think I'll be able to help you in this one, you're delusional."

"Nobody can help me."

"Thank you. I didn't need the responsibility."

"Why couldn't she trust me just a little bit more?"

"It's always been my general belief that trust can take a long time...years, decades, even centuries."

"I forgot. You were married to my sister Joan. You have a good excuse."

"O'Malley's a pretty good excuse, too."

"It's more than just him."

"It sounds like you've got your answers, and I think I helped. I have to tell this to Beth. She'll be pleased."

"I'm not going to her on my hands and knees. She's going to have to come to me on this one."

"You might be waiting a long time."

"That's all right. I'm a patient man."

"Another Scotch? The time will pass quicker."

NOAH WAS SUMMONED home early the next morning. It seemed that bad news traveled fast. He almost ignored the command, stayed in bed with his hangover and dreams of Cassandra. But it was his dreams that caused him the most pain and he was home before he knew it.

After breakfast, his father directed him into the study. "We need to have a plan."

Noah waved it off. "There'll be other opportunities."

"You're not going to fight this? Where's the son I raised?"

"Can we talk about this tomorrow maybe? Or next week?"

Robert beat his fist into his palm. "No. You've got to strike while the iron's hot. Next week it'll be too late."

It already was too late. Goddamn contract. Noah really didn't care. It was Cassandra that was killing him. Noah stood up. "We'll talk next week."

"You never were a quitter, Noah."

No, Noah had always been patient and cunning. He'd bided his time, played the right cards at the right time. Quitting hadn't been his nature, but then, the hole in his heart hadn't been his nature either. Noah needed to get back to the darkness of his apartment. "I can't talk right now."

"This isn't about business, is it?"

Noah rubbed his eyes and headed for the door. "No."

His father followed him and put a hand on the

shoulder. "We're here for you, Noah. When you're ready, the door's always open."

Noah tried to smile, but fell short. "Even for a failure?" That's what had stung. He had been so sure of her, so sure that she finally trusted him. He had succeeded where no other man had. That's the success that he wanted.

"In order to know what winning mightily means, you have to fail mightily, as well."

Noah closed his eyes. "Maybe next week, Dad. Maybe next week."

CASSANDRA WAS SPORTING full body armor when she went to see Benedict the following morning. Her lips were glossed, the tight yet conservative sweater was full of promise. "Look, but don't touch" was the statement she was going for.

It was her fault that Noah hadn't made the list of bidders. She'd hurt his company. In her illustrious past, bad things had happened over her. Noses had been bloodied, eyes had been blackened, relatives had been insulted, but this was the cruelest cut of all.

She didn't waste time with Benedict's secretary, instead she just whizzed right on in. Better to start out on the offensive.

"Why didn't you include him on the list?"

"He's not a known quantity. The contract's too big."

"That's garbage," she said, hands on hips in proper battle stance.

"I make the recommendations. They listen. You really shouldn't have underestimated me."

"What will it take to change your mind?"

"It's too late."

He had always had expressive eyes. They turned sharp brown when he was angry, soft green when he wanted to make up. They were brown now.

She waited for the power to course through her, waited for her confidence to return. She could do anything when she put her mind to it. Noah had told her so. She could even get Noah's bid back. And what would it cost? Nothing that was worth anything to her anymore.

"Aren't you the one who said it's never too late?" she purred.

Benedict, always the sharp one, picked up on the change in her tone. "What are you offering, Cassandra?"

"What'll it take to get him on the list?" she asked, unable to get her tongue around the words she really needed to say.

Benedict laughed. "You're really willing to do this for him?"

There was only one thing she was good for. Sadly enough, this was it. Cassandra turned and locked the door. "It's just sex, Benedict. Don't get excited. The heart has nothing to do with it."

12

NOAH WAS AT HIS APARTMENT when she showed up. He'd been waiting for her. Waiting for her for the last forty-eight hours, waiting for her for the last thirty-four years.

"Hi," she said, her eyes unsure.

"Hi."

"I saw you lost out on the bid."

"Life sucks," he said, now wondering why she was here.

"Can I come in?"

He held open the door.

"I went to talk to Benedict to see if I could sway him to sway the council. It's really easy to get men to do what I want."

"I don't want to hear this," he said, thinking that if she wanted to pay him back, she had picked the most painful way to do it.

"Actually, I think you do." She stood in the middle of the floor, perfectly straight, her arms crossed across her stomach. "I couldn't do it."

He began to breathe again.

Cassandra continued, slowly, haltingly. "I couldn't just have sex anymore. I always kept my body carefully unconnected from my mind, or my heart. When you're only seen one way to the male population, it's easier to just give in, rather than fight."

She was chewing on her lip, and he wanted to take her in his arms and hold her, ease the pain inside her, but she needed to do this.

"You thought too little of yourself."

She continued talking, focusing on some spot right over his head. "I knew he would have done it, too. I could see it in his eyes. It's that mindless desperation. I could have slept with him, and you'd be on that list."

"Why are you telling me this?" he asked softly.

Finally the soft brown eyes settled back to face level. "Because you got mad when I didn't tell you that crappy stuff that happens to me. So I'm going to fix that."

"I don't want the confessionals just to keep me from being mad. I want you to trust me."

"I realized something else today, too."

"What's that?"

"When I saw your company missing from the list, I knew that you'd hurt. And because of that, I wanted to fix it for you. I wanted to help you. To get rid of that hurt. That's how you feel when you're in love, isn't it?"

He nodded.

"What happens to me is usually not pretty, and it's usually not fun, and I hate that you have to see the ugly pieces of my life."

"I don't mind the ugly pieces. I have ugly pieces, too, so does everyone."

"As long as you don't blame me."

"Why would I do that?"

"Well, maybe I don't exactly dress like a nun."

"No!"

"And maybe I know how to flirt with men."

"No!" He began to smile. "Cassandra, I fell in love with that woman."

"Do you still love me?"

"I've never stopped."

"Even if I don't tell you things."

"It seemed like you told me something here today. That counts."

"I did, didn't I?"

"When you hurt, I want to know, Cassandra. Not because I want to go beat somebody up, although I might, but because that's what happens when people love each other."

"How do you know all this?"

"I didn't before I met you. I've been learning right alongside you."

"Really?"

"Really."

"Are we fixed now?"

"Yeah, we're fixed."

"Good."

Just then his phone rang.

"What?"

"Really?"

He started to laugh. "No, I guess I shouldn't be surprised. Thank you for letting me know."

After he hung up, he took her hand. "They've added me to the list."

"Oh?"

"Yes, that was Mrs. Tyborn who called.

"It seems that a small oversight occurred and when the city council was brought in on the matter, they realized the error that had been made, and I was reinstated."

"Oh."

"So, how did Mrs. Tyborn know that I hadn't made the list?"

"I might have said something to her about that."

"Might?"

"Probably."

"I love you, Cassandra."

"I love you, too, Noah."

"Then you're going to have to marry me. Soon."

She looked up, the sly confidence in her had returned, and he was glad to see it in place. "I have some rules..."

Noah shook her head. "Oh, sweetheart, you don't have one rule that I can't break."

And he proceeded to do just that.

Epilogue

THEY HIRED a male stripper for the bachelorette party. It had seemed appropriate at one time in their lives, but unfortunately for the poor college student, nobody was paying attention to him. Jessica had cornered Beth about a recipe for the cheese balls, which they all knew she would never make. Mickey was sending text messages to Dominic, and Cassandra—well, Cassandra was staring off into space.

In less than twenty-four hours she would be married. The word still gave her the chills, but she knew she would be fine. *They* would be fine.

Mickey looked up, noticed the look on Cassandra's face and burst out laughing.

"What?"

"You aren't nervous, are you?"

Cassandra shook her head. Every detail was arranged, her dress was ready, even emergency hair appointments had been made. The ceremony would happen without incident. "You think he's nervous?" asked Cassandra.

"Noah? No way. He's been planning on this for a long time."

Cassandra considered that, and wasn't sure whether or not she liked it. "You think I was a fait accompli?"

Mickey shook her head. "No, just fate."

"Okay, I'll buy that." Cassandra lifted her glass of tonic water to her lips.

Mickey instantly noticed. "Ha! You're not drinking, either. Remember all those 'trying to get pregnant' cracks? You think I forgot them? No way, sister." Mickey stood up and started to call over to Beth and Jessica.

Cassandra pulled at her sleeve. "Sit down. You should know me better than that."

Mickey leaned in and pitched her voice low. "Have you given up drinking on purpose, like me?"

"For another seven and a half months," murmured Cassandra.

"OHMYGOD." Mickey's eyes got wide, especially wide as they were magnified behind really strong corrective lenses. "No one told me. Oh, no! No one knows."

"Uh-huh. Noah doesn't even know yet. I'm telling him tomorrow."

They had a dog. Now they'd have a baby. All right, maybe it made her a little nervous, but she hadn't failed at anything yet. Surely she could handle motherhood. Yeah.

It wasn't exactly the wedding surprise she had pictured, but she wasn't worried. After all, he was the one who wanted to break her rules.

Her smile got a little brighter. That man sure knew how to break rules.

"I have to keep this secret? You can't do that to me, Cassandra. I'm not that strong."

Cassandra folded her arms across her stomach. Very Madonna-like. "Just for another few days. Of course you can handle it."

"No, I can't. I swear I can't. You can't give me that sort of responsibility. You should have told Jessica. She would take it to the grave."

"No, she would have just been sore that she hadn't hit it first."

"Well, yeah." Mickey scrunched up her mouth. "Oh, God. I'm going to cry. Hell, I'm going to be an aunt. Oh, my God, you're going to be a mom." She put a hand over her heart.

Flooded with something she'd never felt before, never known before, Cassandra leaned back and smiled. It was contentment. Contentment born of love. Of being loved. Of loving powerfully in return.

What more could a woman want?

HARLEQUIN®

Temptation.

New York Times bestselling author

VICKI LEWIS THOMPSON

celebrates Temptation's 20th anniversary—
and her own—in:

#980

OLD ENOUGH TO KNOW BETTER

When twenty-year-old PR exec Kasey Braddock accepts
her co-workers' dare to hit on the gorgeous new landscaper,
she's excited. Finally, here's her chance to prove to her
friends—and herself—that she's woman enough to entice
a man and leave him drooling. After all, she's old enough
to know what she wants—and she wants Sam Ashton.
Luckily, he's not complaining....

Available in June wherever Harlequin books are sold.

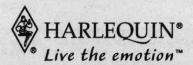

If you enjoyed what you just read,
then we've got an offer you can't resist!

Take 2 bestselling love stories FREE!

Plus get a FREE surprise gift!

Clip this page and mail it to Harlequin Reader Service®

IN U.S.A.	IN CANADA
3010 Walden Ave.	P.O. Box 609
P.O. Box 1867	Fort Erie, Ontario
Buffalo, N.Y. 14240-1867	L2A 5X3

YES! Please send me 2 free Harlequin Temptation® novels and my free surprise gift. After receiving them, if I don't wish to receive anymore, I can return the shipping statement marked cancel. If I don't cancel, I will receive 4 brand-new novels each month, before they're available in stores. In the U.S.A., bill me at the bargain price of $3.57 plus 25¢ shipping and handling per book and applicable sales tax, if any*. In Canada, bill me at the bargain price of $4.24 plus 25¢ shipping and handling per book and applicable taxes**. That's the complete price and a savings of 10% off the cover prices—what a great deal! I understand that accepting the 2 free books and gift places me under no obligation ever to buy any books. I can always return a shipment and cancel at any time. Even if I never buy another book from Harlequin, the 2 free books and gift are mine to keep forever.

142 HDN DNT5
342 HDN DNT6

Name	(PLEASE PRINT)	
Address	Apt.#	
City	State/Prov.	Zip/Postal Code

* Terms and prices subject to change without notice. Sales tax applicable in N.Y.
** Canadian residents will be charged applicable provincial taxes and GST.
All orders subject to approval. Offer limited to one per household and not valid to current Harlequin Temptation® subscribers.
® are registered trademarks of Harlequin Enterprises Limited.

©1998 Harlequin Enterprises Limited

Blaze™

HARLEQUIN® Blaze™

In April, bestselling author

Tori Carrington

introduces a provocative miniseries
that gives new meaning to the word *scandal!*

Sleeping with Secrets

Don't miss
FORBIDDEN April 2004
INDECENT June 2004
WICKED August 2004

Sleeping with Secrets
**Sex has never been
so shamelessly gratifying....**

Available wherever Harlequin books are sold.

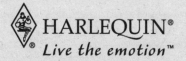

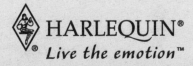